W9-ATW-909

"Get out of here. Now!"

Sam grabbed the backpack. A go-bag packed with essentials for survival, which she'd know meant one thing: they were in trouble.

"Who is it?" she asked, panic in her voice.

He couldn't tell her who. He didn't know. "Put on your vest and let's go." Sidearm in hand, he let her out.

Amy clung to him, her face pale. He wanted to tell her it was going to be okay, but he couldn't. Someone had posted their location on the dark web. His phone was tapped, too. "The red car that followed us earlier just pulled into the parking garage. Our location's been compromised."

He was dark until further notice. In the wind with Amy, no backup.

"I'm going to get you out of this. I promise."

He shouldn't make promises he had no idea he could keep, but Sam steadied his nerves and prepared for flight. This time he wouldn't fail. They were in danger because he'd let his guard down by sinking into his emotions.

If he did so again, Amy would pay for his mistakes with her life.

Jodie Bailey writes novels about freedom and the heroes who fight for it. Her novel *Crossfire* won a 2015 RT Reviewers' Choice Best Book Award. She is convinced a camping trip to the beach with her family, a good cup of coffee and a great book can cure all ills. Jodie lives in North Carolina with her husband, her daughter and two dogs.

Books by Jodie Bailey

Love Inspired Suspense

Freefall
Crossfire
Smokescreen
Compromised Identity
Breach of Trust
Dead Run
Calculated Vendetta
Fatal Response
Mistaken Twin
Hidden Twin

Texas Ranger Holidays

Christmas Double Cross

HIDDEN TWIN

JODIE BAILEY

HARLEQUIN® LOVE INSPIRED® SUSPENSE

If you purchased this book without a cover you should be aware
that this book is stolen property. It was reported as "unsold and
destroyed" to the publisher, and neither the author nor the
publisher has received any payment for this "stripped book."

Recycling programs
for this product may
not exist in your area.

 LOVE INSPIRED BOOKS

ISBN-13: 978-1-335-67903-1

Hidden Twin

Copyright © 2019 by Jodie Bailey

All rights reserved. Except for use in any review, the reproduction
or utilization of this work in whole or in part in any form by any
electronic, mechanical or other means, now known or hereafter
invented, including xerography, photocopying and recording, or in
any information storage or retrieval system, is forbidden without
the written permission of the editorial office, Love Inspired Books,
195 Broadway, New York, NY 10007 U.S.A.

This is a work of fiction. Names, characters, places and incidents are
either the product of the author's imagination or are used fictitiously, and
any resemblance to actual persons, living or dead, business establishments,
events or locales is entirely coincidental.

This edition published by arrangement with Love Inspired Books.

® and TM are trademarks of Love Inspired Books, used under license.
Trademarks indicated with ® are registered in the United States Patent
and Trademark Office, the Canadian Intellectual Property Office and in
other countries.

www.Harlequin.com

Printed in U.S.A.

I sought the Lord, and he heard me,
and delivered me from all my fears.
—*Psalms* 34:4

For Jesus

Who saved me

Who rescued me

Who carries me through

Who delivered me from all my fears

ONE

Rain-chilled wind blew dead leaves across the parking lot at South Georgia Community College, a damp reminder that winter was rapidly overtaking fall. Amy Naylor stopped at the end of a covered sidewalk and stared across the wide sea of vehicles to the far row where she'd parked her midsize SUV. The rain that had poured earlier had given way to clear skies, but the accompanying cold front had dropped the temperature a good twenty degrees.

It figured she hadn't brought a jacket to wear over her navy button-down shirt. Hiking her messenger bag higher on her shoulder, she glanced at the building where her small office offered the warmth of central heat. It would be easy to go inside, make herself a cup of hot coffee and read over the papers she'd assigned her freshmen biology students. For a few more minutes, she could pretend summer wasn't over.

But it was Friday afternoon and the building would empty rapidly after the next class ended in an hour. The long empty halls that echoed small noises after everyone was gone had always forced her out of the building with the feeling that something was lurking in the shadows. She preferred her third-floor one-bedroom apartment, where there was only one way in and one way out. In her home, the couch faced the front door, and no one could sneak up on her through a half-open window. Even her bed was shoved against the wall so she could sleep on her side, eyes toward the door, pistol at the ready in her nightstand drawer.

No one was catching her unaware.

Something buzzed against her side. Amy jumped and threw the messenger bag off her shoulder, then stared down at the gray fabric as she tensed.

Her cheeks heated as the side pocket buzzed again. It was only her cell phone, still switched to silent mode so she could teach her classes without interruption. Not a bomb. Not a kill shot.

Yep. She was going home. Stepping back

inside and pouring more caffeine into her system with another cup of coffee was a bad idea after all. She scooped the bag up by the strap and glanced around, praying no one had noticed her brief dance of panic.

She'd probably never get over the sensation that someone was breathing down her neck or staring at her through a sniper's scope, seconds away from ending her life. Every time she turned the ignition in her car, she held her breath and waited for the explosion that would finally end her life of terror.

The phone had stopped buzzing by the time she retrieved it from the pocket and ducked deeper into the shadow of the building to see the screen.

Seventeen missed calls.

Adrenaline shot through her with a lightning bolt of pain. Seventeen missed calls, all from a blocked number.

No. The word tried to push past the sudden lump in her throat, but fear overpowered it. Only two people called her from a blocked number. And if one of them had called seventeen times in the fifty minutes she'd been in class then, for better or for worse, her entire world was about to splinter again.

Either she was free, or she'd been found.

Both options were equally terrifying.

It took her four tries to dial the number she'd committed to memory three years ago, her fingers missing the numbers, her eyes constantly roaming the area, reading the faces of students and faculty members who were heading to their cars after their just-dismissed classes. No one seemed to be paying attention to her.

The call only rang once before a clipped voice answered. "Amy Naylor?"

"Yes." The voice that had so authoritatively commanded her class only minutes earlier could hardly be called a whisper now, fear choking her into silence. Whatever the voice said next, nothing would ever be the same again. She pressed her back against the brick building and kept watching the flow of students passing by, leading normal lives, certain of where they were headed now that they were free for the weekend.

She envied them.

"It's me. Deputy Sam Maldonado. Are you in a secure location?"

Amy shook her head before it registered that the deputy US marshal on the other end couldn't see her. "Not exactly, but I can get to my office." She turned and headed up the breezeway at a quick clip, feeling as though a million eyes watched her and safety was too far away. She could lock herself inside her office, close the blinds and wait for whatever came next.

"Is Deputy Marshal Edgecombe with you?"

"No." She stopped at the glass doors to the building, her fingers on the handle. If they'd sent a marshal to pick her up, then this wasn't good news. This level of caution and urgency could only mean one thing—her identity was compromised. Her stomach twisted as chills swept her skin. Danger was heading her way, and this was a college campus. If Grant Meyer's people came looking for her with guns blazing…

Her brain wouldn't even consider what might happen to the innocents around her.

Amy slowed and turned on her heel, staring in the direction of the parking lot. Cradling the phone between her shoulder and her ear, she ran her finger absently across the face of her watch, the cracked crystal rough against her finger. "I can't go to my office. There's no way to protect any students on this campus if someone decides they're in the way. And I don't see Deputy Edgecombe." She'd recognize the man anywhere. He stood out in a crowd. At well over six feet, his laughing dark eyes and ready humor belied the seriousness of his job as her contact with the US Marshals' Witness Protection Program.

Along with Deputy Maldonado, Deputy Edgecombe was her first point of contact and had never failed to answer her call or be by her side if needed. If he was supposed to be here, he'd be here. Then again, he was the kind of man to operate under an abundance of caution. It was possible he was waiting in the parking lot for her to exit the building so he could escort her out without causing a scene or raising suspicion. "What's going on?"

"I'm two minutes from your location. Get into your office and get secure and I'll pick you up there."

Maldonado was coming for her? Amy's knees threatened to give way and drop her to the sidewalk. They'd met on multiple occasions, the first only a few months ago when she'd nearly compromised her own identity. It had been her fault that time, for trying to leave Georgia against WITSEC rules. Through a series of coded communications she never should have been involved in, she'd learned that Grant Meyer had gone on the rampage. He'd been hunting down anyone who could testify against him or his human-trafficking ring, including Amy and another witness she'd hidden herself, a young woman in the country illegally who refused to talk to the authorities.

Amy hadn't gotten very far.

Deputy Sam Maldonado was a retrieval specialist, part of the elite team that had been sent to find her and bring her back to safety, fighting to keep her alive so she could testify against Grant Meyer. Since that day, he'd been right beside Deputy Edgecombe, always there and watching, as though he and his team didn't trust her not to run again.

She'd learned her lesson. When Layla Fisher hadn't been at the house Amy had secured for her in Virginia, Amy had panicked. She'd left herself cut off with no protection and no idea of whether or not she'd been discovered. Sam and his team had found her and brought her back to safety.

If Sam was on his way, the Marshals Service was more concerned than his calm voice would ever let on.

"I'm not staying here. It's too dangerous to others for me to be on campus." With quick steps, she headed to her car, fear for her own safety evaporating with the need to protect the students roaming the area around her. "I'm going to my apartment. It's only a few minutes away. You can meet me—"

"For your safety, do as I say." The last four words were heavy with emphasis.

Amy kept talking, her eyes landing on a dark green four-door sedan sitting next to hers. The band around her chest released. "I see Deputy Edgecombe's vehicle. It's parked next to mine. He's here." She killed the call and jogged toward the vehicle, her muscles weak with relief, even as she acknowledged it was only temporary. She was about to be on the run for her life again.

Her feet slowed as she neared the car, the back of her neck prickling with an unease that refused to be ignored. Something was wrong. The deputy marshal didn't exit his vehicle to approach her the way he usually did when they met, always acting cheerful and friendly, as though they were two friends meeting for a social visit. Even then, Amy had read his eyes multiple times and seen them scanning the area for threats.

This time, he stayed in the car. The glare of the late afternoon sun off the windshield tinted the glass red and prevented her from seeing inside, and the driver's side window appeared to be rolled down.

She scanned the line of cars as she drew closer. None of the other reflections off the cars seemed to have that red tint to them.

Her feet rooted to a spot between a sports car and an SUV only a few feet away from Deputy Edgecombe's car. Bile pushed into her throat and almost gagged her. *No. No, no, no.* She clapped a hand to her mouth to hold in the scream as realization hit. That couldn't be blood. It couldn't be. She was rooted to the spot. She should check on Deputy Edgecombe. She should run. She should—

A man stepped from behind her small SUV, his blue eyes locked onto hers, his jaw a hard line as his mouth curved into a slight smile. In his hand, he held a pistol, the barrel pointed directly at Amy's heart.

Amy froze, her eyes on the weapon. She couldn't move. Couldn't scream. Couldn't even blink. This was how it ended, in a Georgia parking lot in the chill of late autumn. This was the price she would pay for doing the right thing.

The man stepped closer and Amy inched one step back. "I wouldn't run if I were you." His voice was low, deep and controlled. "You take off running or try to fight me and you won't be the one I shoot." He kept the gun low, and when Amy tore her eyes away from it to his face, he was eyeing a group of students several rows of cars away.

A sob leaked past her fingers as he closed the space between them, his hand wrapping around her wrist and making her hand throb with the pressure. "You walk with me like we're old friends or I make sure your marshal friend over there isn't the only one who bleeds today."

"I'm thirty seconds out." Deputy US Marshal Samuel Maldonado spoke into his radio and prayed he wasn't too late. He ignored the horns blaring at him as he slowed for a red light then blew through it, hanging a left turn into the parking lot of the small community college where Amy Naylor taught biology.

The past chased him, urging him to push the pedal farther down, to shave away precious seconds. The one time he'd been too late, twenty seconds would have made all the difference.

He couldn't let hesitation wreck another life. Never again.

"Don't call attention to yourself." His team

leader, Deputy Marshal Greg Hayes, was typically a man who kept his cool no matter what the situation. His strained voice in this moment dug into Sam's already frayed nerves. "You have no idea if she killed the phone call or if someone killed it for her. You blaze into that parking lot on two wheels and anyone who's waiting for their moment to snatch her will panic."

As much as it gnawed at Sam to hear it, Hayes was right. They already had one deputy marshal who wasn't responding, even though Amy Naylor had confirmed Edgecombe was on-site. There was no telling what the truth of the situation was.

Sam eased up on the gas pedal and kneaded the steering wheel with both hands, fighting every instinct to move faster. He'd worked with Deputy Elijah Edgecombe for several years, and they'd worked closely for several months, ever since they'd tracked down and reacquired Amy Naylor in Virginia. The woman had actually thought she could take off for a few days on her own. She'd been none too happy when Sam and his team had tracked her down and brought her back to Georgia, and she'd been tight-lipped about her reasons for leaving in the first place. Sam had

stuck close, working with Edgecombe to ensure she didn't run off again. Grant Meyer's
people would be all too happy to find her in
the wind with no protection.

Her saving grace when she'd wandered off
was that Grant Meyer had been in North Carolina, focused on Amy's twin sister, believing
he had his sights on the woman who'd turned
him over to federal authorities and outed his
human-trafficking ring. He hadn't realized
he had the wrong woman until he was behind bars.

Amy's identity hadn't been compromised
then. She'd been safely able to return to her
life as Amy Naylor, adjunct professor in south
Georgia.

Today was a different story.

As Sam broke through the line of trees at
the end of the driveway that opened into the
community college's parking lot, he scanned
the area, searching for Amy's red SUV or
Edgecombe's dark green sedan. He rolled
along the lot, scanning the area. This side of
the parking lot was largely empty, as most of
the students were parked closer to the building.

There. In the next to the last row. The sedan

and the SUV sat side by side. "Got a visual on the vehicles."

"Any sign of Edgecombe or Naylor?"

Sam pressed his lips together and scanned the green sedan. It was too far away for him to get a good look inside, but the red tint of the sun reflecting off the windshield told the story.

The truth came like a blow to the solar plexus. He swallowed hard twice before he could speak. "I don't think he's in a position to offer any help."

Hayes muttered something under his breath, likely words Sam didn't want to hear anyway. "You're sure?"

"Not without getting out to check. Be prepared to call in an ambulance." He itched to park the car and race to his colleague, but he was only one man and a woman's life was in danger. He'd never wanted so badly to be in two places at once. "Where's my backup?"

"Two deputies on the way."

Two people appeared behind Amy's SUV, walking toward a dark gray crossover parked behind hers.

No, that was wrong. The man walked. He was dragging the female along beside him.

Amy Naylor.

Sam stiffened his ankle to keep from pressing the accelerator to the floor. He'd only alert the man and anyone else who might be watching to his presence. Sam had no idea how many associates the man might have, no idea what he was up against. "I've got eyes on her, and it's not good." He relayed the scene to Hayes as he rolled closer. They needed a plan fast, before the stranger shoved Amy into a car and took this horrible show on the road.

Sam didn't dare engage yet. While no one was close to the pair, there were too many students milling in the parking lot and pulling out of the main entrance. They were all in striking distance if the situation disintegrated into a shootout.

Sam was out of options. "I could use some help here."

"Backup is still several minutes out. Can you stall them?"

"I can try." He'd love to call in the police or give the order to clear the parking lot, but without knowing who the man was or what his plans for Amy were, any broad moves were risky. Whatever Sam did would have to be subtle and calculated.

The man who was holding Amy captive was tall, broad and blond. He was bigger than

Sam, though likely not as well trained. He opened the front door of his car and jerked Amy closer.

The front seat. Okay, good. He was likely alone if he was willing to put her in the front seat where she could grab the wheel and wreck the car.

Slipping his pistol onto his lap and holding it at the ready, Sam rolled his window down and pulled to a stop behind the gray car before Amy climbed into the vehicle.

Her eyes widened when she saw Sam. She opened her mouth, then flicked her gaze to the man behind her and closed it again.

Good. If she blew his cover, they'd all be dead.

The stranger slid his hand from her wrist to her back and tried to shove her into the car as he cut his eyes at Sam. "I think you need to keep moving, buddy." His voice was low and heavy with a midwestern drawl. He wasn't holding a weapon, but the way his shirt hung at his side said he had one close to the ready.

Good news? It would take him longer to draw than it would take Sam. Bad news? Amy stood between them—a human shield.

There was an easy fix for that dilemma. He caught Amy's eye, then deliberately looked at the car door, which stood open in front of her. *Come on, Amy. Hear what I'm saying to you.* "I just need directions, man. No worries. You know where the student center is? I've got a meeting with my—"

"I don't know anything." He nudged Amy until she climbed into the car, then he shut the door behind her.

Perfect. Now if backup would get here so they could flank this guy and end this thing without anyone firing a weapon. "I could use a hand here. If you could point me in the right direction, you'd be doing me a solid."

Casting aside all pretense of civility, the man glanced at Amy and strode toward Sam's car, anger flushing his cheeks and narrowing his eyes. "I told you to move. If you know what's good for you, you'll find your gas pedal and use it now."

Before Sam could respond, a black sedan slipped around his car and into the space next to the one where Amy sat, a hostage to her captor. Another sedan slid behind Sam and into the spot on the other side.

Sam almost sagged in relief. Deputy Marshal Vince Wainwright slipped out of his car, drawing the man's attention as another deputy Sam didn't recognize stepped up from the other side.

Amy's attacker reached for the pistol at his side, but Sam lifted his own weapon and aimed it at center mass. "United States Deputy Marshals. And I wouldn't even think about touching that gun if I were standing in your shoes."

The man's head whipped toward Sam and he hesitated, then flicked his gaze back and forth between the three US marshals who had hemmed him in. In an instant, his posture melted from defiant anger to sullen resignation.

Sam's stomach unclenched, but he kept his expression hard. "You're done. Lace your fingers behind your head."

The man obeyed, and the deputy Sam didn't know took him into custody.

Sam eased out of his car and turned to Wainwright. "Deputy Edgecombe's car is right in front of you. I have a bad feeling about what you're going to find." Sam would have checked himself, but Amy was his responsibility.

Deputy Wainwright nodded grimly and disappeared around the SUV as the other deputy hauled their suspect off.

Sam headed straight for Amy. As soon as he pulled the door open, she dropped her head to the back of the seat. "You got him?"

"We did." He had to get her out of here quickly, before any more of Grant Meyer's goons showed up, but she was pale and shaking. She likely needed a minute to gather herself before he tried to move her. It was probable her legs wouldn't hold her until she'd caught her breath. Sam knelt beside her, slightly below her eye level. He rested a hand on her shoulder. "Take a minute. Get your bearings, and then we need to move you."

"This isn't over, is it?"

"No."

"It's bad, isn't it?"

Movement at the front of the car caught Sam's attention. Wainwright, his phone already pulled to his ear, caught Sam's eye, his face tight. He shook his head.

No words needed to be spoken. Edgecombe was gone.

Shoving his emotions to the side, Sam turned his attention to Amy, who was still watching him. "There's a vest in the front seat of my car. When you get in, I want you to put it on." His own was hot under his shirt, but in a retrieval like this, he wasn't taking any chances.

"Deputy Maldonado?" Her face paled, almost as though she'd heard what the two deputies hadn't spoken. "How bad is it?"

He wanted to answer her. He really did. But the truth was worse than anything she could imagine. If he'd arrived forty-two seconds later, Amy's blood would have been on his hands.

TWO

The deputy standing at the front of the car disconnected his call and shoved his phone into a holster on his belt. He seemed to listen to something in his earpiece, then walked over to stand on the other side of the car, watching the entrance to the parking lot.

Amy didn't have to ask about Deputy Marshal Edgecombe's condition. The silent conversation between the two men confirmed her suspicions.

Shutting her eyes against the pressure of tears, Amy did her best to swallow the pain in her throat. Deputy Elijah Edgecombe had been her main point of contact since she'd been relocated to Georgia over three years ago. He'd been the one to deliver news, both good and bad, to answer her questions, to check on her in those dark moments when she was certain she'd never be safe again. He was a good man, although she had no idea what his life outside of their occasional interactions looked like. It was certain someone out there would grieve the loss of a son or a husband or a brother.

If only her phone hadn't been on vibrate. If only she'd answered the first—

"Amy." Deputy Maldonado's hand on her shoulder tightened. "You're okay. We're going to get you out of here."

The other marshal spoke. "Two local detectives are pulling in to secure the scene. Deputy Kline is on his way with a team. Two local officers will escort our suspect out. I'm to follow you. We have to get moving though, before we draw a crowd."

Amy opened her eyes, the full implications of his words bringing the truth back like a slap to her face. Her identity had been compromised. She turned to Deputy Maldonado, who pulled his hand from her shoulder and stood. "I can't go home, can I?"

He glanced at the other deputy, then back to Amy before holding out his hand to her. His brown eyes were sad, either because of Deputy Edgecombe or because of her situation. "I'm sorry."

The adrenaline that had been keeping Amy

upright ebbed and left her entire body aching. Coupled with the weight of what was about to happen, she wasn't sure she could move. She lifted her hand and placed it in Deputy Maldonado's. He helped her out of the car, his support the only thing keeping her on her feet. When the other deputy handed him a bulletproof vest, she let Deputy Maldonado help her into it, the entire scene playing out from a distance.

She grabbed her bag. The other deputy rounded the car and held his hand out over the top of the door. "I'm going to need your bag along with your cell phone."

Amy opened her mouth to argue, then closed it. She'd done this before and had awakened too many times to count in a cold sweat from nightmares that this moment had come again.

Well, this was no bad dream. This was her reality...again. Surrender everything she owned, leave her entire life behind, become someone completely different.

Silently, she passed the bag to the deputy, then drew her cell phone from her pocket and handed it over as well. All she had left of Amy Naylor—and of the real Amy Brady— were the wedding ring she wore around her neck and the antique watch on her wrist. The ring was the only thing she had left of her deceased husband and the watch was the only memento of the friendship that had landed her in this mess in the first place. If her other watch hadn't died two days ago and she hadn't replaced it with this one, she'd have likely been forced to leave it behind.

Amy let Deputy Maldonado lead her to his car. He opened the door and ushered her in, shutting it behind her before he turned to have a quick conversation with the other deputy, the one who was holding what was left of her life in his hands.

With a cold fury, she despised the nameless deputy and she didn't even know him. He represented the horror she was facing. He'd taken the last of her identity away from her. Everything she was, everything that identified her hung casually from his fingertips in her gray messenger bag. The favorite pen she wished would never run dry. The keychain from a hiking trip along the southernmost part of the Appalachian Trail. Her phone with pictures of her few Georgia friends.

Her friends, who would never know what had happened to her. Her students, who would only know that Ms. Naylor never showed up for class. The entire life she'd built here was firmly erased by the taking of her messenger bag.

The bag with a photo slipped inside a torn lining, the photo she wasn't supposed to have in the first place.

"Wait!"

Deputy Maldonado had pulled the door open but stopped before he slid in. "What?"

Amy reached across the seat and grabbed his hand, gripping tight, desperate for him to understand that she needed this one forbidden thing or she might lose her real self forever. "In the top pocket of my backpack, the lining is cut. There's a picture…"

His expression tightened, the *no* already forming on his lips. She shouldn't have mementos like that, pieces of her old life that someone could find and use against her. But she couldn't let this one go. It was all she had left. "Please."

He eyed her for a long moment before he shoved away from the car and walked over to the other deputy. There was a brief conversation before Sam dug through the messenger bag then returned, passing the picture to her as he shut the door and started the car. "I can't promise they'll let you keep it."

"Thank you for trying." She stared down at the photo in her hand. Two women and one man, smiling and happy, in better days when they didn't know that the next two years would rip them entirely apart.

Deputy Maldonado shifted the car into gear and rolled out. He cast a lingering glance in the rearview, likely at the car that held Deputy Edgecombe's remains.

Amy wasn't the only one who was losing today. With a crushing weight in her chest, the grief returned. Deputy Edgecombe's family was about to get a devastating visit. A team of men had lost a colleague. There was a difference in losing a temporary life and losing a permanent one. "I'm sorry."

Deputy Maldonado's eyes shifted to her and he eased out of the parking lot. "For what?"

"About Edgecombe. He was a good man."

"The best." He massaged the steering wheel for a moment, then tipped his chin toward the photo in her hand. "What's so important about that photo that you're willing to risk your neck to keep it?"

Amy turned her eyes to the picture and scanned the faces forever frozen in time. "I can look in the mirror any day and see my twin sister's face looking back at me, but this is the only actual picture I have of her. And it's the only one I have left of my husband and me together."

His head jerked back. "There's no mention of a husband in your file."

"Then you haven't seen my whole file. We were married six years ago, shortly before he deployed to Afghanistan." Amy stared into Noah's laughing hazel eyes. Their entire relationship had been the very definition of a whirlwind. They'd met in January, married in April and he deployed in July. On the first chilly autumn day in September, an army chaplain flanked by two other soldiers knocked on her door. From the first time they laid eyes on each other until the day he died, less than ten months had passed. "He was killed in a firefight in the Arghandab Valley."

"I know the place well."

Amy started to ask how, but experience with the buttoned-down deputy marshal told her he'd only change the subject without answering. While she'd seen him and spoken to him many times, little had changed between them in the months since she'd first met him. Back then, he'd ridden the edge of frustration and anger for the two days it had taken for him and his team to be certain she hadn't compromised her new identity. Deputy Edgecombe had been the one to fill her in on exactly what it was Deputy Maldonado and his people did. An elite recovery team within WITSEC, they were sent after missing or endangered high-value targets in the most desperate situations. She'd gone missing on her own the first time, prompting the deployment of his team. She'd deserved his irritation and annoyance then. This time...

She gasped, guilt burning in her stomach. "Deputy, is all of this happening because of me? Because you had to hunt me down the last time?"

"Call me Sam. We're about to spend a lot of time together, and it will make things easier." Before she could ask what he meant, Sam shook his head. "None of this is your fault. Despite how foolish your actions were a few months ago, no one tracked you then. To be honest, we're not certain what's happening now or how you were found. Our cyber expert was trolling the dark web and found a hit out on you placed only a few hours ago."

"A hit?" It wasn't possible. This was the stuff of action movies and TV shows. How had she landed here? Three years ago, she'd been a normal person working for a living after the loss of her husband, whose insurance money had gone to his mother. She'd wrapped up her degree in sports medicine and was interviewing for full-time jobs in her field. While working on her college job as a personal trainer and part-time receptionist at a day spa, she'd discovered an ugly truth straight out of her worst nightmares.

Her boss, Grant Meyer, had been using New Horizons Day Spa's multiple locations in Texas to traffic human beings. Worse, his partner was a man she'd trusted enough to introduce to her twin sister. Logan Cutter had manipulated Eve until she'd pulled away from everyone in her life, including Amy. When Amy had notified the authorities about the evidence she'd found at the day spa, she never dreamed her life would end up jumping the tracks so completely. She'd been forced to leave everything behind and to become an entirely new person. Certainly, she'd never imagined she'd be the target of real-life hit men, something she'd foolishly thought only happened in the movies.

"Why now?" It had been more than three years since she'd stepped into her life as Amy Naylor. Three years in which, while she never stopped looking over her shoulder, she'd at least grown slightly more comfortable in her skin teaching underclassmen biology at the community college. It was the closest she could come to using her real degree without giving away who she used to be.

"The prosecution is close to securing a trial date. It's possible Grant Meyer was able to make contact with the outside and have you targeted. It seems unlikely, since his organization fell apart after he was jailed and agents rounded up most of his men. Still, if he has any sort of reach, he'll use it to get to you. You're the biggest thing the prosecution has against him. Even though he knows the evidence you turned over is enough to take him down without you ever taking the stand, revenge would be a pretty sweet dish to him. Our big concern is how he was able to tell others where to look for you. And why he'd put out a blanket call for a hit on the dark web where authorities could be tipped off, instead of having someone he trusted come after you. At this moment, none of it makes sense."

The more he talked, the more Amy tensed. Nothing he said made this better. Everything was only getting worse and the crushing weight of it threatened to suffocate her.

Sam glanced in her direction and seemed to notice his words were having the opposite effect of his intentions. "Amy, you're safe with me. I promise. That's why they sent me and why they put my team on the job. No one is going to hurt you as long as you're doing as we—" He tipped his head away from her, to the left where his earpiece was. The lines around his mouth and above his eyes drew tighter and he gripped the steering wheel with both hands, gaze roaming from mirror to mirror.

Amy pressed deeper into the seat, panic threatening to overwhelm her. Whatever he was hearing, nothing good was going to come of it.

Sam eyed the rearview and immediately spotted the vehicle that had sparked Wainwright's concern. The gray full-size pickup had slipped in behind them shortly after Sam merged onto the highway headed toward Atlanta and his team's base of operations three hours and some change to the northwest. The truck hadn't raised too much concern as it had stayed a few cars back and seemed to be running with the ever-increasing Friday afternoon traffic. He kept his voice low, knowing he couldn't avoid Amy hearing him but hoping against hope she wouldn't understand. "You're sure?"

"I'm sure." Wainwright's voice was serious and certain.

Moments like this reinforced the reason Sam liked to travel in pairs and to have someone watching his back during witness transport. There was a reason he liked to have the younger deputy back him up on days like this. Wainwright was competent and quick, with a gift for seeing what Sam couldn't because his focus had to be out the front windshield. "When you hit the highway, the pickup crossed two lanes of traffic and cut me off to stay with you. I don't think he realizes I'm back here, so we have the advantage on him there, but he's definitely latched on to you."

Sam locked his back teeth and scanned the road signs ahead, looking for an exit that wouldn't leave him stranded in the middle of nowhere. They were rapidly heading out of town and would soon be in a broad stretch of pecan groves and onion fields, leaving few places to pull off and hide. "Run the plates and get back to me. I'm going to pull off at the next exit. Sign says there's a shopping mall there. I can make a broad circle in the lot and see if he sticks with me. If he does, there's a better chance of losing him on a side street than there is on the highway."

Beside him, Amy stiffened. Sam wished there was a way to have this conversation out of her earshot, a way to keep her ignorant to the danger, but until someone invented silent speech, that was impossible.

His earpiece hummed as Wainwright spoke. "He'll figure you out the minute you leave the highway. It might make him desperate."

"I know." It was a chance Sam had to take. The guy might spook and back off if he thought he'd been tagged, but it might also make him desperate enough to risk an impulsive move. "Back off enough to keep him from being suspicious of you but stay close enough to keep an eye on him."

"Got it."

Sam checked his mirrors to make sure he was clear, then slipped from the left lane without signaling, abruptly crossing the right lane and taking the exit at the last second.

The truck followed.

"Someone's behind us, aren't they?" Amy had one hand on the grab handle above her head and the other holding tight to the seat beside her. She was even more ashen than she had been before. If Sam weren't already familiar with Amy and her hard-set determination, he'd think she was about to pass out on him. It was a good thing he'd run up against her stubbornness before. She wasn't one to knuckle under easily.

But she was also prone to panic attacks, and Sam couldn't risk one now. From personal experience, he knew they could bring everything to a full stop.

He could skirt the truth to protect her, but in the months he'd known Amy, he'd learned she wasn't one who would believe an easy story. Edgecombe had always spoken plainly to her when she demanded the truth, and Sam would do no differently. When he'd caught up to her in Virginia the first time he met her, she'd smoked him out immediately and demanded he give her the whole truth about her situation. He had. With both barrels. At the time, she'd deserved to hear how foolish she'd been to run off alone.

This time, the fault was not her own so she deserved none of his righteous anger.

But she still deserved the truth.

"It looks like we've picked up a tail, but Wainwright is behind him and our new friend doesn't seem to know it. We're fine. We'll either slip him or we'll call in local law enforcement to keep him busy and shake him off our scent. We're fine." Boy, that had better project more calm than he felt. Adrenaline zipped through his veins. The truth was, the situation could get a lot more complicated. With civilians around and with the driver of the truck being a complete unknown, there were a whole lot of what-ifs that could come to fruition in the next few minutes. More of those scenarios worked against them than for them.

Wainwright's voice buzzed in his ear. "Just got word on the license plate and you really aren't going to like it."

The man had a flare for the dramatic that could make him a little slow with information sometimes, but Sam took the good with the bad. "Probably not."

"Truck is registered to a student at the community college. He was carjacked about the same time we pulled out of the parking lot and called it in. Guy hit him from behind, so he doesn't have a description, but local LEOs are still talking to him. Kid's fine but upset about his truck."

So their original kidnapper had an accomplice. This operation was more coordinated than he'd suspected. Sam balled his fist and hit the side of the steering wheel.

Amy jumped but remained silent.

He'd have to be careful not to scare her any more than she probably already was, which meant he'd have to be careful what he said to Wainwright. Sam waited as cars turned left on the green light into the large shopping center parking lot. "We showed up at the right time to the college."

"Looks like. When we descended en masse, he probably made the wise choice to keep himself hidden. Hayes is having our suspect from the college moved into interrogation now, trying to figure out who the partner is."

In the rearview, the pickup followed Sam into the parking lot, while Wainwright got caught several cars behind him as the light cycled. Sam cruised up the broad center aisle with the pickup still two cars back. At a fork in the drive, Sam hooked a left away from the main lot into a deserted auxiliary lot closer to the road.

The pickup continued straight toward the mall.

Interesting. Far from bringing relief, the truck driver's odd decision to break away amped Sam's adrenaline. Their new friend knew something Sam and Wainwright didn't. "He went his own way."

"You're thinking he's either confident he won't lose you and he's trying to throw you off, or he's got an accomplice who's finally caught up and who's got eyes on you so he's free to move on."

Sam slowed and eyed the cars on the other side of the parking lot. None seemed familiar. He took a second to glance at Amy, who was watching out the front window, her gaze fixed on nothing. She'd detached from the situation and seemed to be watching from a distance.

It might be for the best. According to her file and Edgecombe's intel, she'd started having panic attacks when WITSEC faked her death in El Paso. It had been a concern the last time he'd had to pick her up. An attack at the wrong time could compromise everything. He knew all too well the coping mechanism she was using right now. Detach. Watch the world as though the whole thing was a movie. Don't let emotions creep into the show.

Amy was doing all of that and more. Sam started to ask if she was okay, then thought better of it. The last thing he needed her to do was analyze her feelings before he could get her to a safe place to feel them.

"I'm in." Wainwright's voice cut through his thoughts. "I'm going to come around behind you and see if you've picked up a second tail, although there's no one around you right now."

"Keep an eye out for the first guy." Sam didn't like this. He swung back around toward the shopping mall's entrance. If Wainwright didn't pick up anything else, he was getting back on the highway double time and getting Amy as far from here as possible. Maybe, just maybe, their tail had figured out he was being followed and had abandoned pursuit.

At the end of an aisle close to the road, traffic was nonexistent and no cars obstructed his view. Sam stopped to check every direction and slipped through the cross aisle. Still no sign of the truck and no indication there was another car tailing him. "I'm heading back for the main road."

"I'm going to drop in behind you and follow you out, but I've got a red coupe three aisles over from me trying to mix into the crowded part of the lot. He's paralleling your moves."

So there was another one and he was smart.

He'd stayed close to the building where the parking lot was crowded, blending in with the rest of the cars. He glanced at the rearview and watched Wainwright's car turn onto the row behind him and stop at the same intersection he'd just crossed. "Keep an eye on him. See if he follows."

"Got it. No sign of the truck. I'm going to—" The screech of tires came from Sam's earpiece and from across the parking lot at the same time. Metal crunched with a sickening finality.

Sam hit the brakes and turned to look over his shoulder as Amy screamed.

The pickup had appeared out of nowhere and broadsided Wainwright's car, pushing him at full speed across the narrow intersection and into a light pole. The passenger side was smashed against the truck and the driver's door curved around the pole.

"Wainwright!" Sam yelled for his partner.

Only silence answered.

Sam gunned the engine and spun the car to face the carnage as people raced toward the accident scene. Inside the pickup, the driver was slumped over the steering wheel. The airbag clearly hadn't deployed.

His earpiece came to life. "I'm okay."

Wainwright was breathless but alive. "Get Amy out."

Sam scanned the lot, searching for the red car. To his left, a blur of motion caught the low-hanging sun as the car hung a J-turn and aimed at them, roaring across the empty parking spaces, gaining speed and power.

This was a coordinated attack, and Sam was on his own.

THREE

Amy's shoulder cracked against the window as Sam executed another sharp turn and floored the gas pedal, leaving her stomach somewhere behind them on the asphalt.

"Hold on." Sam's hands were tight on the wheel, his focus on what lay ahead of them. He was intense yet he radiated no stress, only a fierce sense of capability that left Amy with the overarching belief that she was safe. She was safe even inside of a car going way too fast for the empty section of parking lot they were currently speeding through.

There was a brief exchange between him and someone she couldn't hear in his earpiece, but his words didn't make sense to her until he said, "We're going to make a lot of turns without warning."

Amy pressed her back into the seat even farther than she had before. Her fingers ached around the grab handle above the door, but she didn't let go. "Is Wainwright okay?"

"He's okay. Fortunately for him, side airbags are a thing."

Relief was temporary, flung aside as Sam threw the car into another turn away from the more crowded section of the parking lot.

She should have been panicking right now. Her brain should have already given way to adrenaline and fear, throwing her into a state of sheer terror. It had happened under less harrowing circumstances. An overcrowded store during the holiday season. A sharp sound during a movie. Simply waking up too suddenly in the middle of the night. Panic attacks had become a semi-regular occurrence since she'd fled her real life.

Flying across the parking lot as though they'd been fired out of a missile launcher, the only thing she felt was detachment, as though her body was buckled into the front seat but her mind was somewhere slightly to the left. She was two steps behind what was happening.

She braced herself against the dash with her free hand as Sam navigated the turn out of the shopping center and shot up the road toward the highway entrance. Numb detachment was another thing she was used to, a side effect of the anxiety that had hounded her since the night she realized WITSEC had killed the old Amy Brady and given rise to Amy Naylor. Since the moment she'd realized the person she'd been from birth was dead.

In essence, although she still lived and breathed, she'd died that day. No more job. No more friends. No more sports medicine degree. WITSEC had rewritten and recreated her degree. They had fabricated her past work experience to fit this new person, a community college professor teaching biology, which she had studied a bit while taking sports medicine. She couldn't even use her experience as a personal trainer, the job that had kept her afloat during college, without risking her own life. Everything she'd worked for and fought for was gone.

Worst of all, there was no hope of ever reconciling with her twin sister. Like the rest of the world, Eve had been told that Amy Brady was dead.

Well, she would have been told if the Marshals Service had been able to find her. Eve had disappeared shortly before Amy discovered the truth about Grant Meyer and began compiling evidence against him. For all Amy knew, Meyer's coconspirator—who was also Eve's boyfriend—had murdered her... or worse.

Amy jerked her mind into the present, to Sam taking the highway exit and threading through cars like a madman. If she continued down this road of thought, she'd jerk herself out of the numbness and lose control. There was no time for Sam to stop and coax her through an attack now. He needed both hands on the wheel and both eyes on the road.

She stared at her feet braced against the floor mat and prayed her stomach would stay inside her body. Thankfully, she'd never been prone to motion sickness, but a hundred miles an hour on an interstate, weaving between cars, might change everything. "The police won't like this."

Sam's chuckle was low and humorless as he navigated around a slow-moving truck. "My team leader is in touch with them. They'll give us space, but the guy behind us is about to have his hands full."

As if on cue, sirens squealed in the distance, seeming to come from all directions at once. Two police cars zoomed past on the other side of the highway. Amy dipped her head to peek at the side mirror. Two more, lights flashing and sirens blaring, were running up fast on the red car from the parking lot. While Sam and Amy blew past the next off-ramp, the car trailing them cut onto the exit and sped off the interstate, the police close behind.

Sam lifted his foot from the accelerator and exhaled loudly as the car leveled out to a more normal highway speed. His relief was the first sign he'd been holding any tension, a slight crack in his cool armor. He dropped one hand from the steering wheel to his thigh, flexing his fingers as though they were tight.

They probably were, given the grip he'd had on the wheel while he was evading their pursuer. His shoulders, his neck... Everything was probably balled into knots. If Amy had been in his shoes, there'd be a tension headache pounding through her skull.

It was a whole lot easier to think about his physical state than it was to think about all that had happened and all that was about to happen. Denial was her friend, and it would be until she had a moment alone to fall apart. "Thank you."

"Just doing my job." He winked at her, a rare flash of his personality beyond his role as a deputy marshal. There was a flash of a smile, then he tilted his head slightly as though his earpiece was talking to him again.

The glimpse of the real person who lived inside of him zinged along her spine. Amy looked away. It wasn't as though she hadn't noticed him the first time she'd seen him, the epitome of tall, dark and gorgeous. Every time he'd visited alongside Deputy Edgecombe, Sam had dogged her thoughts for days after.

She'd ignored the attraction. Her minor in psychology had taught her to recognize that her childhood could create a fascination with honorable men and heroes who galloped in on white horses to rescue fair maidens.

The men in her young life had been transient, coming and going at her mother's princess-fantasy whims. Her mother had been addicted to the rush of new love. The minute her high was gone, she moved on to someone else.

Only one man had stayed longer than a month. Only one man had ever come close to being a father figure, and he'd vanished when his connections to organized crime threatened Amy and her sister.

She clenched her teeth. Amy had promised herself she'd never be like her mother, drift-

ing into the princess fantasy of needing a man
to rescue her or to complete her.

As it turned out, she was almost as bad
as her mother. She'd jumped into marriage
with Noah when she was nineteen because
he'd not only loved her but had promised
the security her life lacked. They were both
young, lost and looking for someone to come
home to. Sure, she'd loved him, but maturity
made her wonder what would have happened
with their marriage had he come home alive.
They'd still been in the getting-to-know-each-
other phase when she'd married him. Like her
mother, she'd fallen into the rush of first love.

She wouldn't make the same mistake again.
If she remarried, it would be to someone she'd
known for longer than a month.

With a glance at Sam, she created another
resolve. If she ever remarried, it would be to a
man who didn't make her feel special simply
because he'd rescued her from the gnashing
teeth of a human-trafficking dragon.

"You doing okay over there?" Sam's voice
cut through the memories and dragged Amy
into the reality she'd been trying with partial
success to avoid.

"I'm fine." A dull ache in her knees and
fingers reminded her she was still braced for

impact. Painfully, she unwrapped her fingers from the handle above the door and shifted her legs from side to side to relax her knees. "Where are we headed?"

Sam drummed his thigh and the steering wheel with his thumbs. "We're going to my team's headquarters in Atlanta. It's secure. You'll be safe. While we're there, you'll be briefed on everything that's happened and someone will go over your options with you. In a few hours, you'll know more than I do."

That probably wasn't true, but she'd act as though she believed him. "Last time, when the marshals faked my car accident, I was in a safe house in Ohio for a few days." It had been horrible. The place had been a nondescript cookie-cutter rental home in the middle of a small residential neighborhood. "I was stuck in a back bedroom with the blinds closed for days. All I had was a TV and some books one of the deputies picked up at a grocery store." Used to regular physical activity both in her personal life and on her job, she'd craved a run or a good set of weights. The tension had overwhelmed her and, without release, the panic attacks had come on stronger each day. That first run she'd taken after her relocation had been both terrifying and liberating.

Sam cast her a sympathetic smile. "I'm afraid this won't be much better. It might even be a little bit worse because you won't be in a house, at least not at first. I suppose when we turn you over to a relocation team, you'll be in a safe house again for a short time, but for a day or so you'll be stuck with us in an industrial office building." He grimaced as though he were silently apologizing. "We do have a couple of rooms with some temporary sleeping quarters. Cots actually."

Great. She already missed her king-size bed with the down comforter and the memory-foam mattress cover. "You realize I have nothing on me, not even a toothbrush. I didn't even get to grab my go-bag or my EpiPen."

"Your go-bag?" His smile quirked higher, then faded. "You actually kept a bag packed in case you had to run?"

"It's in the hall closet, a duffle bag with some clothes, papers, things I wanted to hold onto, ready to grab if you guys ever knocked on my door and said it was time to go. I never expected you to show up at my job and rip my life away without warning."

Sam winced, but he didn't reference the last

comment. "I'm sorry you have to live life on edge like that."

"It's not your fault."

"Well, when it comes to the EpiPen, we can get you a new one, but I have one if the need arises before that. Let's just say that bees are not my friends."

"Same. Along with bee pollen, oddly enough. I took some once as a supplement and it almost killed me." She'd only had an allergic reaction one time, but not having a shot at the ready made her edgy. "I'll tell you right now, I bear some contempt for the marshal who took my bag. It's like he stole..." She sighed. It was as though he'd stolen her identity. Again.

"I could tell you he's a really nice guy who has a wife and kids, but it won't help, I know." He clicked on the blinker and turned onto another highway. "There's a female marshal, Deputy Dana Santiago, on my team. She'll make sure you have the necessities you need for the next few days. Much like the last time, you can give us a list and a team will go into your house and try to retrieve what they can. We'll get some of your stuff to you as you start over again, but I'm afraid it won't be much."

She knew the drill. She wished she didn't, but she did. As far as the rest of the world was concerned, Amy Naylor no longer existed.

For the next hour, they rode in silence. Sam spoke little, listening to the back and forth in his earpiece as his team coordinated with other members of the Marshals Service and tried to piece together what had gone wrong. No one seemed certain who had leaked Amy's whereabouts or how she'd been found. No one could give intel on how many bad guys were on the hunt. The men they'd taken into custody refused to talk, more afraid of whoever was funding them than they could ever be of the marshals.

In the silence, Sam fought to keep his emotions at bay. A strong sense of relief came with the word that Wainwright had been released with minor injuries after his dustup in the shopping center parking lot. The suspect who'd rammed him had been arrested, and a team was at the shopping mall, scouring surveillance footage from parking lot cameras and security feeds for other suspicious vehicles.

As expected, other news wasn't so comforting. In the midst of a recovery operation was not the time to give in to grief, but the call that Edgecombe truly was dead had come as a blow. Sam had known, but hearing the suspicion clarified in stark, no-nonsense words hadn't been easy. It would have been nice if he could pull over and take a second to pull himself fully together.

He needed to get his head on straight, but he couldn't afford the luxury. Priority number one was to get Amy to headquarters. After that, he could sit down and debrief, then grieve with others who had known Edgecombe, or who at least knew what it was like to lose a brother-in-arms.

In the rapidly fading evening light, they raced around the city of Columbus. Only an hour left. He flexed his fingers on the steering wheel and checked the rearview again. Since they'd evaded the red car, his eyes had roved from mirror to mirror, searching for a tail, watching for signs of danger. So far, so good. If he could keep her safe for an hour longer, he could hand off Amy to his team and relax in the knowledge he'd saved her from a criminal intent on killing her.

Amy shifted in the passenger seat and stretched her legs, pulling her neck from side to side. She had to be tense and tired. There had to be a million questions running through her head, but she hadn't said a word in over an hour. She'd merely ridden in silence, alternating between stillness and restless fidgeting.

The silence in the car was too loud, leaving him too much room to think about all that had transpired today, on the most disastrous mission of his WITSEC career. Today's destruction rivaled some of the carnage he'd experienced overseas with his Special Forces team. He'd never dreamed he'd bear witness to such loss at home.

Sam had to break the heavy silence, get a conversation started or something. "We're almost there. About an hour more."

She nodded but didn't look at him. She was probably thirsty, starving or any number of other uncomfortable things. Pulling over for a drink and a burger would invite trouble. While he felt certain they'd left their pursuers behind, there were risks he simply couldn't take. Unlike some of the witnesses Sam had retrieved, Amy hadn't complained or loosed an angry tirade. She simply stared out the front window, silently accepting her fate.

Reality likely hadn't kicked in for her yet. When it did, the fallout would not be pretty. That wasn't for Sam to deal with. Good thing.

Sam had never been stellar at helping people deal with their emotions. WITSEC had psychologists and counselors on staff to handle the mental and emotional ramifications of going into hiding. With her life in shambles for a second time, Amy was definitely going to need a session or two.

"Did you ever talk to anyone about your husband?" Sam winced as soon as the question left his lips. Seriously. There was making conversation and there was prying into places he had no business digging. Keeping his mouth shut would have been the better option.

There was something about this woman though, something that made him feel as if he knew her better than he did. Maybe it was because he'd spent time with her when Edgecombe checked in on her. Maybe it was the way she'd opened up to him earlier in the day. Or maybe it was simply who she was. Amy was different than any other woman he'd ever encountered, on the job or off.

She was definitely different than his ex-wife.

"My husband?" Her voice had a hazy edge to it, as though his question had drawn her from somewhere far away.

"Never mind."

She stared out the side window and said nothing for a couple of miles. "No. I didn't."

So she had caught the question after all. "Was there a reason you didn't?"

"I talked to my sister. I never saw the need to say anything to anyone else. It hurt when Noah died. I lost him, my future, everything. Even the apartment I was living in, my car..."

That couldn't be right. The soldier in Sam remembered all of the paperwork he'd had to fill out prior to a deployment. Points of contact for notifications, burial instructions, beneficiaries for life insurance... The whole morbid list was as long as his arm. Things no one wanted to think about when they were headed into a war zone but things that had to be squared away to ensure the protection of their loved ones at home before they could go wheels up to do their jobs. "How is that possible? You should have been taken care of. There should have been so much available to you." There it was. Another way too personal comment he never should have made.

Amy shook her head, her blond hair spilling over her shoulder and swishing against her cheek. She tucked it behind her ear. "We got married so fast. He never changed his paperwork. I guess he never expected to die. Who does?"

Sam's heart sank. As a single soldier, all of his benefits had been directed to his mother and father. Amy's Noah had likely done the same in his single life. And if their marriage had happened on a timeline as tight as the one she'd indicated, he'd already filled out his deployment paperwork and had likely not even considered the consequences of not changing beneficiaries.

She was right. What man wanted to consider his death, especially when he was trying to cram in as much living as possible with a brand-new wife?

"I wasn't even his primary notification on his paperwork. I found out what happened to him because one of the chaplains in the battalion knew me. His parents got the notification. I heard secondhand. I'd never met his family. They lived in Puerto Rico." She sniffed, then swallowed and turned away from him. "I didn't even have the money to fly to San Juan for my own husband's funeral. I've never even seen his grave."

Sam's heart shattered. He gripped the steering wheel tighter to keep from reaching for her hand, which would have been a decidedly unprofessional move. When she said she'd lost everything, she wasn't exaggerating. Had she even felt she had the right to grieve?

For long miles, he didn't know what to say, how to soothe the ache she was bound to feel at her husband's death and his family's slight. The woman beside him was stronger than he'd imagined. "So you never talked to anyone except your sister?" It was the best he had to offer, and it was completely lame.

She didn't seem to notice. "I didn't want to fight his family, because I figured they had even less than I did. And nothing was going to bring him back to me, so why bother talking to someone about it? It was going to hurt no matter what."

"And yet you minored in psychology."

She cast him a rueful glance, her eyebrow quirked. "That was in my file too?"

At least she was somewhat smiling. It was better than heated anger or chilled silence. "Yep."

"WITSEC wouldn't let me do anything that even remotely smelled like my career goals or the work I was doing at the gym to pay my way through college. Truth is, I had enough biology to be able to teach at the community college level since I studied sports medicine. I was accepted to grad school so I could become a physical therapist and work with athletes. A psychology minor made sense so I could dig into a bit of how the mind works so that I could figure out what made an athlete tick, could help them recover from an injury in body and in mind, maybe even in spirit."

"That sounds kind of New Age."

"Far from it. It sounds like Jesus. A lot of athletes who are injured, especially at the levels I was shooting for, have their whole lives change when they're injured. Entire careers get derailed. Dreams die. There are psychologists and counselors for that sort of thing, but I know a lot of people talk to their physical therapists and open up more on the table than while sitting on a couch in a counseling session. I figured I should know something about how to help someone whose world has been completely rocked and their dreams shattered in a way they never saw coming." She trailed off and ran a finger along the stitching in the seat between them. "I never realized when I was taking all of those classes that all those things I learned would apply to me someday. Or that I'd never get to use my real training.

I got to gather up all of my knowledge and teach instead."

"Has teaching been that bad?"

"I've actually enjoyed it, but I miss me. I miss having goals and plans and dreams. It's been three years and I've never figured out what I want to do with this new life. Good thing, since it's gone now too." She pulled her hand into her lap and balled her fists between her knees. "Maybe that's why I never came up with a new dream, because some part of me always knew this day would come and it would all be snatched away again."

"I'm sorry." He truly was. Somehow, this whole detour in her life felt like his fault.

"Thanks, but you're trying to protect me. This is Grant Meyer's fault. All the more reason to see him locked away forever."

Sam exhaled a breath he hadn't even realized he'd been holding. Sometimes, when things got too heated, a witness would back down and decide not to testify. While Amy had turned over enough evidence to condemn Meyer without her testimony, federal prosecutors needed her to be willing to testify if any questions came up about those documents and how she'd obtained them.

"I have no regrets about my decision to

turn my boss over to the authorities. A lot of people were freed from a terrible man's clutches." Her expression turned pensive, and she fingered the antique watch on her wrist. The leather band was scratched and worn, and the crystal over the gold face bore a small crack near the bezel. "I just hope they got far enough."

"There something special about that watch?"

Amy blanched, her cheeks going pale as she laid her hand over the watch's face as though she could hide it and possibly even erase it from Sam's memory completely.

Something was very wrong here. He'd merely asked because the way she absently ran a finger across it made it appear to be some sort of security blanket. He'd thought it might have belonged to her husband or someone in her husband's family. Now, his radar pinged on high.

Innocent people didn't have things to hide. The way she was protecting that timepiece, there was no doubt…

Amy Brady was hiding something big.

FOUR

"Talk to me, Amy." Sam's voice had shifted away from friendly sympathy and had taken on the hard edge of the federal agent he was.

Shifting, Amy cradled her arm against her stomach, palm still pressed against the face of the watch. She was fully aware she looked like a small child who'd been caught with her hand in the cookie jar and was trying to hide the evidence.

Why had she even touched the watch in the first place? When she entered the program, WITSEC had cleared it as an item she could bring with her. It was simply a watch, a family heirloom. There was no secret to the piece itself.

The secret was in the history behind it. Spilling the story to a federal marshal would likely get her a slap on the wrist, but it could completely destroy the lives of two people she cared about and needed to protect.

Defensive words and arguments built in her chest until she could feel them trying to force their way out, but that posture would only make him more suspicious. Instead, she pulled in a deep breath, swallowed the angry words and faced him head on as though she had nothing to hide. "I have literally had my entire fake life ripped away from me today. Everything. Even my favorite pen that I found in the faculty lounge one day and have guarded like the treasure it is ever since." She paused, but Sam didn't rise to the bait of her attempted humor. His jaw was still set with a tightness that spoke of his suspicion. "I just don't want to risk someone taking this away from me too, even though I have permission to have it. It's literally all I have left of anything that used to be me." While she hadn't told the whole truth, it was close enough. So close that the sting of tears burned her eyes.

The tension in Sam's jaw eased. "It was your husband's."

Amy turned away and stared out the side window as the exits grew farther apart and the traffic decreased outside of Columbus. Let him think that. If he found out the watch had really belonged to Layla's great-grandfather, she'd have to reveal who Layla was. To tell the truth would put the marshals on the hunt for the younger girl as a potential witness, one of the many young women Grant Meyer and Logan Cutter had trafficked. The one who had led Amy to realize the truth about her boss and New Horizons. The woman had "worked" with Amy at the day spa. When Amy learned that Layla's "job" was actually Grant Meyer's way of exacting pay for sneaking her illegally into the country, it had been the catalyst for Amy reporting her boss's behavior. Amy had been the one to help Layla disappear into safety.

Layla was the only one Amy had been able to help escape the traffickers' clutches.

Amy wouldn't risk Layla being found and possibly exposed to the kind of fear and uncertainty that Amy herself had lived with for the past three years. The girl had been through enough.

Sam laid a hand on her shoulder and the warmth nearly undid what little reserve she had left. He pulled away nearly as quickly as he'd touched her, as though she'd scalded him. "For a minute, I forgot what today must be doing to you. What the past few years must be doing to you actually."

What it was doing to all of them. Though Amy had been unsuccessful in tracking Layla down in Virginia, she'd prayed daily for the young woman's continued safety and continued anonymity in a place Grant Meyer could never find her. She had no idea where to find Layla or how to start looking but...

What if protecting Layla meant telling the truth? Sam had tracked Amy down almost as soon as she left the state. What if he could find Layla and bring her to safety as well? Amy ran her thumb over the watch crystal, knowing she stood on the edge of a point of no return. "Can I ask you a question that stays between us?"

"Depends on the question."

At least he was honest. "What if I knew of someone out there on their own? Someone Grant Meyer might be looking for?"

Sam's head jerked toward her, his eyes searching her face before he dragged his attention back to the road. "Who?"

Should she do this? Possibly send the authorities after Layla? If she was found by federal authorities, she could be detained or deported. Meyer had brought her into the country illegally along with dozens of other women like her.

"Amy, if someone's in danger, I need to know about it." Sam passed a slow car and eased back into the right lane again. "Is this about your sister?"

"Eve?" Pain seared through her, the grief always close to the surface. "I don't even know where Eve is or even if she's still alive. She vanished before I went into WITSEC and I have no way of knowing if she ran from Logan Cutter or if he…" It was a thought she never allowed herself to complete.

Amy had been the one to introduce her sister to the handsome businessman who delivered and maintained the equipment at New Horizons, a day spa that included a gym and personal trainers in the mix. If she'd only known the darkness that lurked behind those all-American blue eyes and sun-bleached blond hair. That monster had groomed her sister, had slowly eased her away from everything and everyone she loved until he became her whole world. Amy's twin sister, who had been her best friend her entire life, had turned away the moment Amy suggested that Logan might be involved in something too hideous to imagine. Whatever had ultimately happened, wherever Eve was, Logan had already stolen her forever.

"Wait." Sam's voice sliced through her pain. "When you took off back in the winter and I found you, you weren't going to your sister?"

"I never said where I was going."

"But you were headed north."

What difference did her direction matter? She'd been on her way to meet Anthony Reynolds, the man who'd been a father figure to her, the man who'd helped Layla disappear and had likely saved her life. He'd contacted her via a coded message on a website out of California, revealing that Meyer was on the hunt.

She'd never reached Anthony. Sam had tracked her down only a few days after she headed out. Anthony's next message had told her to stay put, and then he'd fallen silent.

But if Meyer had found Amy, then it wasn't a stretch to believe he could find Layla too. "I was on the way to warn someone else, someone Grant Meyer might see as a threat."

"Another potential witness?"

Amy nodded once.

"Who?"

"You can't approach her. Not without me. Don't send your team in."

"I can't promise—"

"She'll run, Sam. She'll bolt before you can get to her and then she'll be totally alone. If you can find her, promise me you won't approach her without me. If she runs..."

"Who is she?"

Here it was. Decision time. If she truly trusted Sam, she'd trust him with Layla's secret. "She was a victim of Meyer's and a friend of mine. It's because of her that I started putting the pieces together. She tipped me off, and then I started digging. Sam, she's a friend but she's also in the country illegally. If she thinks the authorities are after her, she'll run rather than be deported."

"Name."

"When I hid her, we changed her name to Layla Fisher. A friend helped with the logistics of making her disappear." Amy had tried to search the name on a public computer once, afraid someone would be able to trace her search, but she'd found nothing. Maybe Sam could locate her, and they could move her safely.

"A friend of yours?"

Amy nodded once, refusing to say any

more. Anthony's activities could land him in jail for a long time. He'd made a living by hiding criminals and forging new identities, a WITSEC for criminals, if the truth be known. He was a master at his chosen profession, and his ties to organized crime had ultimately been the reason he'd left Amy and Eve and their mother behind.

Sam kept his attention on the road as he spoke into his earpiece. "Reach out to our contact. You know who I mean. We need the location of Layla Fisher. Just a location. No movement until I make the call." He listened, then glanced at Amy as his voice lowered. "You heard what I said. Do it."

He navigated in silence, seeming to consider something for several miles. Finally, he seemed to come to a decision about whatever was rolling around in his head. "We need to talk about something. Your—" He stopped, his head doing that tilt thing it did when his earpiece went active. Sam had both hands on the wheel, his eyes scanning the mirrors in a way they hadn't since he'd left the driver of the red car behind them a couple of hours earlier.

Instinctively, Amy turned and looked behind them. Although it was too dark to make out anything other than headlights, traffic was light. No car seemed to be following too closely. "Tell me what's happening, Sam."

He held his hand out, palm flat. He was still listening. Whatever he was hearing must be incredibly detailed and very bad news. The way his forehead wrinkled and the lines around his mouth and eyes tightened didn't bode well for her.

"Copy." He watched the road ahead as though he didn't actually see it but was instead reading something in his mind. With a heavy sigh, he slid the car into the far right lane as soon as he had an opening in traffic. Without using his signal, he took the next exit, toward Warm Springs and Pine Mountain.

If they were still headed to Atlanta, this was the long way. Amy's heart pounded against her rib cage. This stank of a sudden change in plans, an off-the-cuff detour that meant something on the other end had gone terribly wrong. "We're not going to Atlanta, are we?"

"We are. We're just taking the scenic route."

"Because…"

He didn't look at her. "Because I said so."

If she was going to survive this, she needed

some semblance of control. "Don't start lying to me now. We've come too far today for you to start hiding information about my own safety from me."

He navigated a turn as the car wound up a gentle slope into the rolling mountains of the southern Appalachians. "Okay. Fair enough. About a quarter of a mile back, there's a deputy marshal trailing us. We picked him up about half an hour after we lost Wainwright."

At least they weren't as alone as she'd feared. But if Sam was making a detour, then the other deputy had spotted something of concern. "What's the rest of the story?"

"Four or five cars in front of him is a silver SUV. Could be something, could be nothing, but he's hung on for the last forty-five minutes or so. Instead of staying on the highway, we're going to make some extra turns through the back country and see what happens."

"So you chose the mountains. With sharp turns, drop-offs and all." Amy kept her voice level, but her mind raced through a thousand ways to die in the Georgia mountains during a rapidly darkening fall evening. Over a guardrail, down a cliff, into the mountainside…

Jerking her head to the side, Amy tried to

force away the images of the car tumbling over and over to the base of a rocky slope while she and Sam tossed inside like abandoned socks in a dryer.

Sam seemed to read her emotions. He laid a hand on her shoulder, then withdrew it to the steering wheel. "Trust me."

His words sank in and calmed the storm raging inside of her. Since she'd settled into the front seat of this car, she'd done nothing but trust the man beside her. It could be because he was a familiar face in the midst of chaos. Or it could be the otherworldly confidence he seemed to exude, as though nothing Grant Meyer threw their way could phase him. Either way, she took a deep breath and released it. Sam wouldn't let anything happen to her. She had no doubt. He was simply too mission-oriented to fail.

Trust me.

Had he really said that to her? Not only did it make him sound like a B-movie hero, it implied a promise Sam wasn't certain he could keep. This entire operation had spun out of control. One good man was dead. Another was injured. No matter which way he turned, it seemed the bad guys were on his tail.

The silver SUV had taken the exit right behind them. When Deputy Utley followed, the driver took off to the south. With Utley in pursuit of the suspect, Sam was on his own.

It seemed the bad guys knew exactly where Amy and Sam were headed and were determined to stop them before they arrived. On the road they were vulnerable, and Sam was torn between keeping a low profile and calling in the cavalry to escort them to Atlanta. At this point, he wasn't even certain whether to continue on to rendezvous with his team or whether to head for a safe house to try to throw Meyer's people off the scent.

His radio came to life and severed his line of thought. Dana Santiago, his second-in-command and their tech specialist, sounded grim. "Our informant's on the line with me. He won't give us any information unless we provide him with some first. He wants us to confirm that your passenger is safe and is with you. Apparently, he's managed to get wind that something went down with her today, but I don't know how he knows."

This was tricky. Amy's retrieval was a closely guarded secret within WITSEC. Only Sam's team and a handful of deputy marshals who'd been handpicked and given information on a need-to-know basis were involved. Some of the deputies providing backup only knew they'd retrieved a witness and had no idea who Amy was or her importance to the Grant Meyer case. His informant was a man named Anthony Reynolds, who'd been working with the US Marshals for years in return for documents that kept him in business helping criminals disappear. Sometimes, he helped them disappear straight into custody. Reynolds had known Amy's family for years and had been instrumental in the capture of Grant Meyer when he'd targeted Amy's sister, who now lived under the alias Jenna Clark in the mountains of North Carolina.

Until half an hour ago, Sam had been unaware that Amy was completely in the dark about her sister's fate, and now he had no idea what to do with the information he held. He'd nearly told her the truth, but Utley's interruption had given him time to reconsider. Amy was already insistent about this Layla woman. He didn't want to know the trouble she'd give him if she found out her sister was still alive and thriving. Eventually, the truth would come out, but hopefully she'd be out of Sam's hands at that point. If not, she was likely to strangle him or, worse, look at him as though he'd betrayed her.

Holding onto the information shouldn't have twisted his gut into knots. It was routine for his team and other deputy marshals to distribute and withhold information when necessary. He'd never felt guilt over it before.

He'd also never felt personally invested before. His continuous presence in Amy's life over the past few months had messed up his head and he needed to get his brain reoriented to tactical thinking instead of letting his emotions dictate how he did his job.

Dana's voice came through his earpiece again. "Is this Layla Fisher a potential witness?"

The prosecution was desperate for more witnesses. The information Amy had collected was more than enough for a conviction, but more was always better, especially with snakes as slippery as Grant Meyer. "Yes."

"Is she worth the risk of letting the informant know the truth?"

"Yes." Anthony Reynolds had never given any indication that he wished either of the Brady sisters harm. In fact, from all reports from both him and the sisters, the girls were the closest thing the man had ever had to real family. He'd been the one to hide Amy's sister away from Logan Cutter, providing her with a new identity. "Tell him and then get back to me with a location."

"Your people can find Layla that fast?" Amy spoke for the first time since they'd started their climb into the hills.

It was a touchy question, one he'd have to be careful about answering. While withholding information was one thing, lying to her was another. For some reason, he felt obligated to be as honest with Amy Brady as he possibly could while still protecting the integrity of her case. "My people are well connected." He slid her a sideways glance. "How do you think we found you the first time?"

"You put a tracker in my shoe?"

"No, but if you run off again, we might." He chuckled in spite of the situation. She was trying valiantly to keep things somewhat light. He'd follow her down that trail if it kept her from panicking on him. They couldn't stop this train from rolling right now, even though no one was trailing them at the moment. "Skill. You made two big mistakes when you went looking for Layla."

"Yeah?" She turned toward him, backing

herself against the door and adjusting her seat belt. "What were they?"

"The first was renting a car. I get that you were trying to keep us from following yours, but it's pretty easy to trace a rental."

"Once you get a warrant. That takes time."

He tipped his head toward her. She was smarter than he was giving her credit for, and that probably wasn't working in his favor. "Admittedly, that slowed us down a bit. Of course, you probably counted on that."

She was looking awfully smug over there. There had to be a way to wipe that smirk off her face while maintaining the lighter tone the conversation had taken. She'd need the humor if his plans kept going the way he feared.

"So, what was my second mistake?"

"Easy." He settled back in his seat as though this were a pleasant cruise through the evening, relaxing a bit as they made their way onto flatter ground. "Your second and biggest mistake was taking off when it was my team tracking you. You didn't stand a chance."

"Wow." She crossed her arms and stared out the side window past him. "Okay then. Glad to know you're a humble man."

He grinned and prepared to fire his carefully prepared witty comeback, but Dana's voice in his ear stopped him. "You're not going to believe this."

"Try me." It couldn't get much worse. Pretty much nothing had gone his way today. He braced himself to hear that Meyer had already found Layla Fisher and had done away with what he certainly perceived to be a loose end. He prayed he wouldn't have to inform Amy that her friend was missing or worse.

"Anthony Reynolds is somewhere off the grid and no one's been able to reach him, but another contact says he stashed Fisher in Toccoa, but she vanished when Meyer went on his rampage a few months ago."

"Come again?" Toccoa, Georgia, was less than two hours north of Atlanta and less than three hours from his current position. A witness had been living practically under Sam's nose and only hours away from Amy.

If she was missing though, it was likely Meyer had found her before he was arrested. "Let Watkins know ASAP. The deputy marshal in charge of his team would want this information as soon as possible. Have him get the team based in Virginia on it. They're our next closest resource."

"No." Amy's hand gripped his arm so

quickly Sam nearly jerked the steering wheel. He'd almost forgotten she was in the vehicle. "If you're going to get Layla, I'm going too."

"Hang tight, Dana." He left his mic hot as he shot a heated glance at Amy. "It's not what you think. And even if it was, you're in danger. My job is to—"

"So is she." Her fingers dug tighter, as though she could somehow get him to understand if she left bruises behind. "She will run. Do you get this? She'll either fight you and end up dead or she'll take off and hide. If she does that, no one will ever find her again. You can't put her in the wind that way, Sam. I have to go."

"No." He packed every inch of his authority into the single word. He should tell her the truth, that Anthony hadn't made contact, but she didn't need more stress. Feeling the slightest pang of guilt, he pulled his arm from her grasp before he turned his attention back to Dana. "Let me know when you get the all clear. My ETA to you remains the same, and we'll proceed from there."

Amy withdrew and crossed her arms over her chest, her chin dipped low. She wore a glare that could melt the windshield. He knew her well enough to know this wasn't a retreat.

This was her working up a full head of steam so she could argue with him all the way to headquarters.

Sam steeled himself against the storm brewing in her countenance. This was his team. She was his mission. He called the shots. The target on her back was big enough to have the Marshals Service activate his elite team in the first place. She had to trust him and understand he had her best interests at the center of everything he did.

He couldn't risk more lives lost because of him. He had enough to atone for already.

Amy had faced ample danger for one day. The sooner she was off the road and in protective custody, the sooner he'd breathe easier and be on to his next retrieval.

They were losing altitude quickly in the rolling mid-Georgia mountains as they headed toward 185 and Atlanta. He'd had enough of wandering through the backcountry. His radio had gone silent, likely having issues with the terrain. This was the part he hated. The part that tensed his muscles because he was totally alone, exactly the way he'd been alone when Devin Wallace had been killed on his watch.

The same couldn't happen to Amy.

His fingers tightened on the wheel as he took another curve as fast as he dared in the near-darkness. All he wanted was to hand her off to the relocation team before—

Headlights flashed and grew brighter, the sudden high beams forcing Sam to wince and turn his head.

There was a car in his lane.

Heading straight toward them.

FIVE

Amy stifled a scream and threw her hands in front of her face, instinctively bracing for impact.

Or for her worse nightmares to come true as they tumbled down the side of the mountain.

Sam jerked the wheel and the car swerved to the right, the rock face so close Amy could touch it if she rolled down her window.

She tore her eyes from the sight as they hugged the mountain, staring out the front window. Sam was headed straight for the car, unable to move any farther over in his lane.

The headlights grew closer. The passenger mirror scraped rock as loose gravel flew up from beneath the tires. Sam didn't slow. Didn't swerve. Didn't look to the right or to the left.

He was playing chicken with her life, hoping whoever was in the other car would blink first.

If they didn't...

Amy squeezed her eyes shut, seconds feeling as though they stretched into hours. If the other car didn't flinch, the head-on collision would kill them all.

She held her breath.

Tires screeched. Rubber burned. The car jerked, then picked up speed as a loud crash crunched behind them.

Amy opened her eyes. The only light came from Sam's headlights on the road as he pressed on the accelerator and pushed them along the mountain's ridge.

Sam was speaking into his radio, his voice pleading. "Come on... Come on. Give me a signal."

Whipping to look over her shoulder, Amy caught sight of the other car resting against a tree at the start of a curve. It had missed the guardrail by inches, saved from going over the edge by a tall pine.

She planted her palms on the dashboard, trying to ground herself as Sam grabbed his phone and checked for a signal before dialing, only one hand on the steering wheel as he navigated his way around the twists and turns of the mountain at a truly terrifying speed. Amy locked her elbows and dug her feet in to keep from being thrown from side to side.

"I've got no radio signal, and we've got trouble." He detailed the incident and their general location, ordering someone to call the police and an ambulance and to "get help on the road now." Finally, he listened, nodding as though the other person could see him. After several turns that nearly threw Amy against the window, he killed the call and dropped the phone into the cup holder without saying anything. There was a tension in his jaw, one that told her he'd not only passed on some distressing information, he'd received some as well.

"What's happened?"

He held up a hand, then shoved his sweater up to his elbows, focused on the road. "Give me a minute."

Instinctively, Amy shrank against the door, the words hitting like quick, clipped blows. Time spun and looped on itself.

If the way his voice had deepened and his forehead creased during that phone call hadn't clued her in, the breakneck speed he was hurtling along the road would have told the tale.

"You didn't have to snap at me." It was the first thing that came to mind. Stupid, but better than focusing on the bigger truth—for all of the precautions Sam had taken today, her life had once again come very close to being extinguished.

He drew his eyebrows together. "You're right. I shouldn't have." He tapped the wheel a few times and navigated a couple of turns. "Forgive me for forgetting my manners when someone just tried to drive us off the side of a cliff."

Okay, so neither of them were at their best right now. Given his job, he should be used to this.

She was not. "Don't lie to me. What else is going on?"

"I'm not a hundred percent sure."

"Then why are you bound and determined to make sure I die on the next turn this road throws at you?" Control. She needed control. Their speed was the least of her worries, even if her stomach was threatening to run for the next county. No, this lone-wolf marshal was serving up her worst nightmare on a rusted metal platter in the cab of his dark gray sedan.

The reins of her life had been wrenched

from her grasp the moment she'd chosen to reveal the true business happening behind the scenes of the day spa she'd managed in El Paso. Now, someone had located her in her new life and was determined to destroy her. This flight up and down the mountains highlighted a stark fact... She had no control. Not over where she was going and not over how fast she got there.

Her heart pounded faster, pulsing through her like a drumbeat. Her thoughts spun. Her breaths pumped harder. She couldn't fill her lungs, couldn't get enough air. Couldn't process what was happening. For all that she'd been numb earlier, the panic now broke over her in waves. Nowhere was safe. No one was safe.

She had to run. The vest over her clothes was too hot, too tight. She wanted to claw it off her body so she could breathe.

Desperate to escape, Amy snaked her hand toward the door handle, heedless of the warning shriek in the back of her mind that the car was moving too fast and she'd die if she made the leap.

It didn't matter. Someone already wanted her dead, and now the marshals were going after Layla because of her. She had to save herself. She had to save Layla. Surely she could run faster and farther on her own, outside the prison of this metal death trap. She needed to be free and to breathe fresh, moving air.

The world hazed gray as she jerked, the panic taking total control. Her left hand jammed the button on her seat belt as her right grasped the door handle.

A strong arm slammed against her chest, knocking her against the seat as the car skidded to a stop in the middle of the road, fishtailing slightly, headlights shining at a ridiculous angle across the low hills in front of them.

"Have you lost your mind?" Sam's voice was a roar. "If you have a death wish, I want to know now before I risk my life for you again."

Amy clawed at his arm, digging her fingernails into his sweater, frantic to escape. If she stayed in this car, she would die. So would Layla. They'd all die.

They'd all die.

When Sam released her, Amy shoved out the door, but the smack of cold air and the surrounding darkness stopped her. She turned left, right. There was nowhere to run. No escape.

Strong hands grasped her shoulders, holding her steady. "Look at me. Right now. Look. At. Me." The words were authoritative yet gentle, commanding her to meet his eyes.

Sam's face was shadowed by the headlights at the front of the car, but there was enough illumination to see dark concern in his eyes.

"Good. Watch me." He breathed in deeply through his nose, then out through his mouth. "Do what I do."

Cold sweat heated her skin as fear cooked through her. Amy fought to stand still, to center her attention on Sam and to shut out the monsters in the darkness. One shuddering breath in, one out.

In. Out.

Sam nodded. "Again."

Five or six breaths later, Amy closed her eyes. Her heart settled. Her mind reconnected to her body. The panic dropped to a manageable fear.

"Okay." Sam's hold on her shoulders eased, though he didn't release her. "I promise it's going to be okay."

Amy's muscles gave way and she slid down the side of Sam's car, sitting against the tire, dropping her forehead to her knees. She'd almost grown used to the way fear leaped out of the dark like a rabid coyote, striking when she least expected, taking over her senses and driving her into flight. The first panic attack had hit the night federal marshals had faked her death, the moment she'd realized how irrevocably her life had changed. There was no reset button, no way to return to what she'd left behind. She would never be herself again, never reunite with her twin sister, never chase her dreams.

The panic had sprung up again and again over the years. No one ever knew what to do with her when it happened. But Sam… "How did you know how to help?"

He kicked a stone off the side of the road, then walked to the rear of the car and stared in the direction from which they'd come. He paced past her again, looking to where they were headed, patrolling, watching for danger. His movements were like some of the soldiers she'd met at the gym in El Paso. Systematic, rigid, trained.

It was a long moment before he spoke. "We can't stay here. There's no telling if that guy has friends waiting around the next turn. We have to get moving."

When her muscles felt as though they could hold her weight, Amy reached up, grabbed the base of the side mirror and pulled herself to stand. She reached for him as he passed, her fingers around his wrist. "How did you know what to do?" She laid each word out slowly, emphasizing the syllables, refusing to let him ignore her.

"Been there, done that."

Amy dropped his wrist. Nothing about Sam Maldonado made him seem like the type to lose control. All evening, he'd held the reins, had been completely in charge. Even now, pacing and watching, he seemed larger than life, his broad shoulders and the muscles evident in his back and arms an outward show of capability. The idea of him losing control the way she had…

Fear melted into embarrassment. She'd lost control. Completely. Sam ought to leave her on the side of the road to freeze to death. It would save her the trouble of dying from humiliation.

"You okay now?" Gone was the friendly man who had talked with her on the highway and distracted her from her fear. Gone was the compassion that had helped put her back together a few minutes earlier. In their place was a federal marshal ready to move out and complete his mission.

Amy nodded once, even though he wasn't looking at her, then slid into the car and buckled her seat belt.

The car rocked when Sam slammed his door, but he proceeded at a slower speed. He drove several miles and made a handful of turns along back roads in silence until he reached a deserted gas station and pulled off behind the building, killing the lights.

The darkness across the hills was complete, thick clouds hanging low to obliterate the stars.

Amy pulled her thin sleeves over her hands, trying to make herself small. "Why are we stopping?"

"Because you need a minute to catch your breath and I need a minute to wait for my people to catch up to us. We're less than an hour from Atlanta and this is getting out of control." He shoved the car into Park but left the engine running. "We're relatively safe for now, and I can get out of here easily if I have to. We're waiting on a next step." He glanced at her. "Local law enforcement is coming in to offer an escort. Unmarked cars, more people watching before and behind us." Sam didn't look at her as he laid out the plan. Instead, he seemed to be hiding.

He was keeping something from her. "You still haven't told me what's changed. Whoever was on that phone call told you something."

"I don't think you should worry about—"

"Don't." In the aftermath of panic, boldness took over, fighting for control so that fear couldn't stage an encore performance. "The conversation was about me. I deserve to know."

"Fine." Sam pressed his palms against the steering wheel, his expression unreadable. "It was my team leader. Whoever is after you has a motive we can't figure out yet."

"You can't say that. It's Grant Meyer. He wants me—"

"No. It's not." Sam faced her, his eyes dark and flashing something that might be anger. "Grant Meyer is dead."

Sam should have found a better way to tell her, should have given her a little bit of buildup or warning before he informed her the man responsible for her life's destruction was not the same person who was now trying to wipe her off the planet. A small transgression in the grand scheme of things, but one more reminder of how easy it could be to miss the mark.

He knew how fragile life was, how quickly someone in his care could be ripped from this world.

Sam jerked his chin to the side, trying to shake free the unbidden vision of Devin Wallace, bloodied on the ground by a bullet fired in a drive-by shooting.

A camera on a convenience store across the street from the shooting had told the tale. Sam and his team had been forty-two seconds too late. Forty-two seconds marked the time between a man's life and his death.

It was a number he'd never forget, especially since Devin's brother, Xavier, had confronted Sam outside of his office the day he'd packed up and left his job to join this team. *My brother's blood is on your hands. You cared so much about yourself that you couldn't even spare forty-two seconds to save his life.* The other deputies on Sam's former team had intervened, pulling Xavier Wallace aside, but Sam had never forgotten the grief and hatred in the other man's eyes.

Hatred Sam deserved.

The woman beside him was still alive, although Sam had no idea if her forty-two seconds had started ticking already. He hated this, sitting behind a burned-out gas station on the edge of a field with only a handful of escape routes, waiting on an escort that might take forty-two seconds too long to arrive.

He had to shut down the countdown clock in his head. Dragging his focus into the present, he turned toward Amy.

His current assignment sat beside him in her seat, frozen. She didn't blink, didn't flinch, didn't even seem to be breathing. Instead, her eyes were fixed on something outside of the vehicle and she simply stared, a sudden statue that Sam had to protect at all costs.

As her eyes widened, understanding shot through him. Sam reached across the car and grabbed her shoulders. "Breathe, Amy. You have to breathe." He'd seen this before. Shock, panic or some other high emotion smacked a person sideways, then their brain shifted out of survivor mode into processing the intel.

With a shuddering gasp, Amy inhaled and whipped around to face Sam. She gulped air and stared at him as though she were trying to comprehend if this was reality, if she was wide-awake or trapped in a very cruel nightmare.

Once again, he demonstrated for her what

to do. "Breathe with me. Come on, Amy. I don't have a paper bag if you're going to hyperventilate on me here."

She choked on a laugh and turned away. It was possible she was hysterical, or maybe his off-the-cuff sarcasm had somehow been funny enough to break through. If she thought he was a laugh riot, she was worse off than either of them had imagined.

Amy breathed a few more times, her lips rounded as she took in air and released it again.

Sam lost track of his own breathing while watching her. The close air in the car, the adrenaline rush of a life-threatening chase... It all stirred his emotions, swirling them inside his stomach.

No. It wasn't the danger or the brushes with death. It was Amy herself. Since he'd flown to her rescue a few months earlier, she had never been far from his thoughts. Every meeting with her and Edgecombe had left him wishing for more. Sam had held his silence and been stoic during those encounters, but it was mostly because he was full of questions about her, wanting to know who she really was, how she really ticked. There was something about the way she drew her shoulders back and faced whatever came after her. Something about the way her situation might throw her into a spiral for a moment but she always fought back, stronger than before. Those green eyes spoke to him, sometimes showed up in his dreams.

Yeah, no. He'd been down that road before and he'd paid a heavy price when his ex-wife couldn't stay faithful. There wasn't room for relationships in his life. Wasn't room for a woman who distracted him from the job. He was gone too much and in too much danger too often, exactly the same as he'd been when he was married to Lindsay. This job was all-consuming, and he wouldn't drive down that road again.

Even if the scenery was beautiful.

He dropped his hands from Amy's shoulders and sat back in his seat, letting his fingertips rest at the base of the steering wheel, giving them both space to reset themselves.

Amy found her equilibrium first. "Grant Meyer is dead?"

"He was murdered." Someone in the prison where he was awaiting trial without bail had managed to get a run at him, using a home-made knife to stab him in the neck.

"I thought he was in some sort of solitary,

away from the rest of the population or something so he couldn't reach out or make any contacts."

"He was. Apparently, this happened a few hours ago so the authorities are still trying to piece together what went down." It could have been a typical behind-bars beef. Traffickers weren't always treated kindly behind prison walls, not by other inmates who viewed them as lower than even murderers on the scum scale. Another prisoner could have gotten wind of who he was and taken justice into his own hands.

It was better than the alternative explanation: that someone had targeted Grant Meyer, someone who was trying to clean up whatever mess they perceived he'd made, someone who was making a power grab in order to rebuild an organization that had been left in shambles when Amy turned over her evidence and agreed to testify.

That scenario would be infinitely worse, because it would mean whoever had had Meyer killed was the same person trying to take Amy out of the equation, trying to tie up Meyer's loose ends in a bid to restart the organization with a clean slate. It would mean that whoever was out there was a big fat unknown and that prosecutors were going to have to start from square one.

It meant Sam and his team would have no intel on who might be after Amy, how they operated or where they might strike next.

They needed to get to Atlanta and his secure headquarters now more than ever. Sam leaned forward and scanned the road, searching for lights, listening for sounds. He needed that escort, fast. He took in the field before them, deep blue in the moonlight, and tried to scan the shadows. They probably couldn't hide for long.

"Does this mean I'm free?" The question, thin and tentative, looped a noose around Sam's heart and pulled it tight. Amy saw light at the end of the tunnel and thought it was hope—freedom from a life of lies on the run.

Sam wished she'd waited until they were in Atlanta before she asked that question. He didn't want to be the one to have to tell her the light was a freight train carrying volatile nuclear explosives.

He rolled through a dozen different ways to cushion the blow, to put off the question or pretend he hadn't heard her. In the end, he couldn't deny her the truth. "No."

It was a simple answer, the best he could

give her when his intel was thin and his communication was spotty. It was both freeing and binding, speaking with honesty yet snuffing the light on her one candle of optimism.

"Oh." Amy barely breathed the word and, while Sam wasn't looking at her, he could sense the defeat. She slumped as though her spine had given out and left her with nothing for support.

Hope dashed. What was that verse his mother used to say? Something out of Proverbs, something about lost hope making a heart sick. Maybe if he'd listened closer, he could offer Amy something more than a crushed spirit right now.

Her pain seemed to take on a life of its own in the car. It practically whispered to his own hidden pain, reminding him of how it had felt when he'd realized Lindsay wasn't going to change. That there was no longer any hope for his marriage, that his entire future with all of its goals and dreams and plans had shattered, slicing him into ribbons and leaving him to stare at a dark void.

No one had been there to reach for him when he'd stepped into an empty apartment after that last brutal deployment. An empty space devoid of furniture, of Lindsay, of anything.

Well, he was here now when Amy was suffering, and he wasn't about to let her have to straighten her spine alone when he could give her something to let her know he'd been there too, that he'd have her back until the end of this.

Or at least until the Marshals Service pulled him off her case. His hand eased across the seat. His fingers laced with hers, uniting them—her in her current desperation and him in his past pain.

He could ask to be reassigned to her case, to come off the constant running that was witness retrieval and stay put for a while, making sure Amy Brady got what she needed to survive until her tormentor was caught.

He could make her a promise and try to take the blackness away from this moment, to give her something to hold onto, something solid in a world that had twisted into more uncertainty than she even realized.

Sam opened his mouth to speak, but a light broke the darkness down the road, then another. His radio crackled to life. "Local LEOs have you in sight." He bit down on his tongue and leaned forward, searching the road. Two unmarked SUVS and two unmarked sedans pulled into the parking lot, maneuvering until there were two before him and two behind them.

His promises could wait until another day. For now, he pressed pause on the forty-two second countdown and prayed Amy would survive whatever surprise struck them next.

SIX

Amy sat on a thin metal cot, elbows on knees, head in hands and focus on the floor. Half an hour ago, after a mercifully quiet drive to the outskirts of Atlanta, a vehicle switch and a winding drive through traffic, Amy had asked to be alone.

Sam's team had complied, giving her the promised windowless "guest room" in the office tucked into a high-rise near downtown. From the outside, the ninth-floor space appeared to be a nondescript consulting firm.

The inside was far different. In this office, lives hung in the balance, shielded by Sam and his elite team of deputy marshals.

The introductions had been brief and her walk through the office quick, but Amy knew the tall, willowy brunette Sam had introduced as Dana was a tech genius. She'd emerged from a room filled with laptops, large screens and the hum of servers. The AC had blasted Amy's arms as she'd passed, a clear indicator that equipment was working to the max.

There was also Isaiah, a six-foot-something wall of muscle. Amy wasn't sure she wanted to know his job description, but she was certain she wanted him on her side.

The other three faces and names blurred as Sam ushered her up the hallway into the small holding room. His relief at having her safely ensconced in his headquarters had been palpable as his shoulders relaxed and his demeanor eased. He'd been all-business as he shut the door behind him, leaving her with her requested quiet.

Other than the small cot, this room smelled, felt and looked like a business office, right down to the is-it-gray-or-is-it-blue Berber carpet.

Maybe it was gray. She turned her foot so her shadow shifted. No, blue.

She'd been playing this game for ten minutes, trying not to think about the implications of what Sam had told her in the car.

Grant Meyer was dead. Murdered. Whoever had killed him hadn't tried to make it look like a suicide. She knew the brazenness of the killing was what worried Sam and his team. She'd been in WITSEC long enough to know Meyer's murder was a message. *I can find you anywhere. No one can stop me.*

Now that she was alone and the adrenaline was wearing off, thoughts assaulted her no matter how much she tried to avoid them. Her mind had gone on the attack in the quiet, when the only sound was the soft hum of voices from somewhere down the hall. Sam and his team were plotting their next move, devising the best way to protect her from an enemy who was a ghost.

A light tap on the door brought Amy to her feet, her pulse jumping. They'd found her. She was about to die.

Then again, killers typically didn't knock. They charged in and took what they wanted without bothering with politeness. She winced, cheeks heating at her fear. It was probably Sam, stopping to check on her.

His presence shouldn't make her heart continue its rapid dance. Maybe she was freaked out over the possibility he was coming to take her away. Even a cot in a windowless office was better than fleeing in the dead of night.

Another tap, followed by a feminine voice. "It's Dana."

Dana. Not Sam. Her shoulders dropped.

"Come in." Amy shoved her hands in her pockets as the other woman slipped into the room and shut the door behind her.

Dana moved with the grace of a ballet dancer, although she was dressed in jeans and a gray polo that bore the logo of a company that didn't exist. Isaiah's shirt had the same logo. She extended a bottle of water. "Sam being Sam, I figure you haven't had anything to eat or drink. He's on his way with snacks until we can get something more substantial. There's a Filipino restaurant down the street that makes the best *lumpia* you ever tasted."

In answer, Amy's stomach rumbled, the mention of food reminding her that she'd taught through lunch. "Thanks. If I'd known how today would go, I'd have done more than grab a muffin at the coffee shop for breakfast." She cracked open the bottle and took a long draw. "What's *lumpia*?"

Dana grinned as though they were old friends reuniting for coffee. "They're like Filipino spring rolls. You'll be on the hunt for more every time you get hungry. Sometimes when you're not."

"Good to know." There was an undercurrent in the conversation, something Dana wasn't saying, as though this girl talk was about to reveal something that would bring on another bend in the road. Amy took a cautious sip of her water and waited, trying desperately to project calm, knowing she probably looked as awkward as the outcast geek in an '80s teen movie.

"So…" Dana leaned against the wall beside the door and crossed her arms. "I'm guessing you know I'm not here to talk about amazing fried bundles of food joy."

"I figured."

"Sam's tied up in a logistics session while Isaiah fills him in on some intel. I was sent to ask you a few questions."

Mimicking Dana's posture, Amy crossed her arms as well, the water bottle damp and cool against her side. "Like where I might want to resettle?"

Dana winced, then shook her head. "I'm sure that conversation is coming. I'm sorry it has to happen to you again, but no. They sent me to ask about the past few months, if you remember anything unusual, any people taking a sudden interest in you or strange occurrences at work or your apartment."

"None that I can think of." Amy ran her finger around the face of her watch, tracing the crack in the crystal. "Nothing stands out."

It wasn't as though she socialized a lot. Sure, she had a small circle of friends, but having to hide her entire past made deeper relationships tricky. She'd long ago resolved not to date, not wanting to lie to a man about who she really was, afraid she'd slip in conversation and reveal everything.

"Any of your students take a particular interest in your class, ask for some extra one-on-one time during office hours?"

Amy shook her head. She'd have definitely noticed that. As one of the younger adjuncts at the community college, she was careful about how much time she spent with individual students, wary of implying a friendship that wasn't there.

"Okay, let's talk about your friend Layla. What's your—" The door eased open and hit Dana in the shoulder. She stepped forward as Sam eased around her.

"Sorry." He looked a bit sheepish. "Isaiah's looking for you. He's trying to pull up a map on the secure server."

Throwing her arms out, Dana whirled on one heel as though she'd forgotten Amy existed. "I've told him a dozen times not to touch those machines. He does something to mess them up every time and it takes me a month to restore everything the way I like it. I think he does it on purpose." She disappeared out the door, gesturing as she talked, her running dialogue about Isaiah and his lack of tech awareness staying away from her stuff.

Sam leaned out the door and watched her go, chuckling. "Always fun to set her off." He was still smiling when he turned back into the room, that grin doing something squirrelly to Amy's stomach. "Oh, hey. I brought you a snack to hold you over until the real food gets here. If Dana's involved, it will probably be from the Filipino place up the block. I think she's addicted." He held out his hand, producing a pack of orange peanut butter crackers he'd probably found in a vending machine.

"Thanks." Amy took the offering before she sank onto the edge of the cot. Settling the water bottle on the floor, she stared at the crackers, the sight of them resurrecting memories she'd buried when the need for her new identity and new life story had overtaken her past. So many memories. So many emotions. All in a stupid pack of crackers.

Amy swiped at her eyes and ripped open the plastic. She popped a whole cracker into her mouth and let the salt sprinkles dissolve on her tongue, certain she wouldn't be able to swallow past the ache in her throat.

"Wow." Sam sat beside her, the cot sinking with him. "If I'd known crackers could move women to tears, I'd have been more careful with my choices."

A swig of water, more chewing, more water… Finally, Amy was able to swallow. She turned the package over and over in her hands, a couple of neon orange crumbs drifting to the ambiguous blue-gray carpet. "I haven't had these since I was in high school. My sister and I practically lived on crackers, peanut butter sandwiches and coffee back in the day."

At the mention of her sister, Sam tensed and eased a bit away from her. He cleared his throat. "You've hinted before that your early life wasn't easy."

"No, but we made it work. Our mother was the kind of woman who chased after any man who could promise her happiness. As soon as things got difficult with whoever her current flame was, she'd bail. It was her way to simply vanish with the man-of-the-month and leave us on our own. She chased happiness with men, but she never had the joy to back it up, never would give her life to Jesus."

"What about your father?"

Amy chuckled, but it held no humor. "Clearly, my birth certificate is not in that all-knowing file of yours. If it was, you'd see a big fat bunch of nothing where my father's name should be. I can't give you one single piece of information about him. I don't know if my mother wasn't sure who he was or if she'd moved on from him and didn't want him involved." She brushed cracker crumbs from her pants. "We were sixteen when she died, and we petitioned for emancipation instead of going into the foster system. We'd been taking care of ourselves for so long it seemed easier. By then, we were both working while going to school and we actually had more than we had before she died. We had each other too. Until…" Until Amy had decided Logan Cutter was dashing and friendly and charming, the perfect man for her sister.

Oh, how wrong she'd been. It had been a swift decline as Logan convinced Eve she needed no one but him, that he loved her, that he'd take care of her… By the time Amy figured out what was happening, the man had emotionally abused and manipulated Eve until the sisters were separated for good, the gulf between them wide. Eve cut all ties with

Amy, her mind twisted into believing that Logan truly cared and that Amy only wanted them to be apart. And now, Amy had no idea where her sister was or even if she was still alive.

Sam stood and paced the room, stopping at the door to look down the hallway in the direction Dana had taken. His shoulders were straight, his posture stiff, as though there were some burden he'd picked up when she started talking.

Amy stood. "Sam? Is there something you're not telling me?"

He exhaled loudly and turned to her, his expression tight and his eyes not quite meeting hers. "I think there are a few things we need to talk about while we're here, before we move on to DC and get deep into the relocation discussion."

"Okay…" Whatever it was, it must be a hard truth. For all they'd been through tonight and in the past, she'd not seen Sam look quite this tortured.

"You may want—"

"Sam!" Isaiah's voice echoed up the hallway, his deep bass seeming to fill the room.

Sam stepped backward out the door and looked toward the sound, morphing from uncertain bearer of unknown news to confident deputy US marshal. "What?"

"Dana needs you. Now." Isaiah stopped at the door and glanced in at Amy. "It looks like she found the data breach and it's not good."

Sam shoved past Isaiah and bolted from the room, calling over his shoulder to his teammate, "Stay with Amy until I get back." In no way did he want her out of that room. He needed to control what she saw and heard until he could tell her the truth about her sister.

He slowed and stepped through the door of Dana's office. The room was larger than the conference room and housed more computer equipment than most big-box electronics stores. Large and small monitors filled the space that also held their internal servers and processing equipment. A separate air system kept the space cool to accommodate all of the equipment and to keep it from overheating. There were no chairs because Dana typically paced as she worked, her way of thinking and ramping up her step count in the daily competition the team had devised to keep them connected and competitive when they were scattered across the Southeast.

When Sam walked in, she turned from the monitor she was looking at and aimed a finger at it. "I don't know how, but someone just used Edgecombe's login."

Sam reached for the large metal bar-height table that dominated the center of the room, the steel cool beneath his fingertips.

"I'm not sure. His login should only work on his machine, because the system recognizes IP addresses and only allows the ones we've white-listed." Dana turned to the monitors, her fingers working over the track pad on the table before her. "I'm in the process of scanning his recent logins, trying to see if there's a pattern. It's possible some of the times he appears to have logged in to the system, it was actually someone using a cloned version of Edgecombe's machine. There are notes on Amy Brady in the system. If someone found a way in, they'd know everything about her."

Straightening, Sam closed the distance between him and Dana, watching the screen as she scrolled. "Can you see the location of the machine that's on now?"

"That's what I'm digging for. If we can get that info, we might be able to find out who your bad guy is before he can strike again."

"Does the system know Amy's here?" If it did, they'd have to move immediately, and Sam was certain she wasn't physically or emotionally ready.

Dana shook her head. "No. Her movements since you picked her up haven't been logged." Her eyes never left the screen. They simply moved back and forth as she scrolled through lines of data, her brow furrowed. When she shook her head, Sam's stomach bottomed out. "Every single login has been authenticated by the IP address, including the one that's accessing the servers now. Someone has their hands on his laptop."

Sam drummed his fingers on the metal table. "No. His entire vehicle including his laptop was secured at the scene."

"Then someone was able to spoof his IP address on another machine. I can check and see if there are overlapping logins, though the system shouldn't allow it."

"I need you to find that machine."

"I can track it as long as it stays online but that could take a few minutes, and we have to hope whoever's looking doesn't know that. On the flip side, we have to hope they don't stay on too long, because that would mean they're getting deep into information we don't want them to. Edgecombe's access was limited to his people, but still… On the dark web, data on the handful of hidden witnesses he's handling could go for big bucks to the right bidder." Dana dropped her hand from the track pad to her side. "Sam, I can remotely shut this guy down and knock him off the system, but that kills any chance we have of tracking him."

Sam scrubbed his hand on the back of his neck. If they let their bad guy stay in the system, Dana could locate him. But the longer he lingered, the more data compromised and the more people whose lives might be in danger.

This was bigger than Amy. It was bigger than Sam. Bigger than all of them. He dropped his hand to the table with a thunk. "Shut him down."

Dana didn't hesitate. A few swipes on the track pad, a few different screens, then she stepped away from her machine with an oddly defeated sense of triumph. "He's off. And probably mad as all get-out. Worse, he knows we're onto him."

"We kept him from breaching more data. Take the win. Let's notify the deputy who's taking on Edgecombe's caseload. Have him contact his people and make sure they're okay. Put a watch out on the dark web to make sure nobody's name surfaces. And is there a way for you to track the usage on Edgecombe's login and get a data history? See if you can find out what this guy learned and where he was in the system?" What Sam didn't know about computers was a whole lot more than what he did.

With a sly smile, Dana turned her back to him and walked across the room to another monitor, swiping her finger across the track pad to wake the machine. "I'm amazing, Sam. I can do anything given enough time." She hesitated. "I may even be able to track down the spoofed laptop, assuming the bad guy doesn't rip out the hard drive or dump it into a river somewhere." Her voice was grim. She wanted to find the guy. This was personal to all of them. Deputy Edgecombe may not have been on their team and he was, in fact, a stranger to everyone but Sam, but he was still one of them—a deputy marshal killed while doing the selfless job of protecting another person's life.

He should have gone with Edgecombe today instead of waiting to be called in. Like Devin Wallace, Sam had been too late. He wondered if forty-two seconds had been the difference in Edgecombe's life and death as well. He balled his fist, digging his nails into his palm, desperate for a physical pain to drive way the emotional hurt. "Work fast."

Dana stopped moving. "Deputy Edgecombe's death isn't your fault. Neither was Devin Wallace's."

Sam froze. How did she do that? Dana could read him as easily as she read computer code.

But she was wrong. "You can't say that."

"I can." She faced him, her expression serious. "Edgecombe was doing his job. And Devin Wallace made a bad choice by setting up a meeting with someone from his old life. That's not your fault."

"I should have been there."

"Then you and your team would have been killed in the crossfire."

Sam looked away. Dana was amazing with what she did, but she dealt in black-and-white code, not in real world flesh and blood.

"Sam, you're not God. Only He knows when our end comes. You don't have any control over that."

Enough. Much more lecture, and he'd crack. Sure, God was in charge, but He'd also called Sam to protect, and Sam had failed.

Twice. He knocked his knuckles on the table and edged toward the door, desperate for some levity. "Get me what I need to take down this guy and I'll keep you in *lumpia* for a year."

Dana looked like she had more to say, but then she smiled. It didn't quite reach her eyes. "Now there is some supreme motivation. And Sam? You should feed the lady down the hall." Dana leveled her gaze on him. "She's a strong one."

"She is." Stronger than any witness he'd ever dealt with.

"She seems to be handling this well."

"Better than most." Sam angled toward the door. He should check on Amy. For all that Isaac was as friendly as could be, he was also quiet. Quiet paired with his sheer size could make him menacing to people who didn't know him.

"She's pretty too," Dana said.

"Very." *Wait.* Sam's head jerked up. "I mean, I guess she is. I hadn't noticed."

There was a knowing look, the one that almost made him question why he was friends with someone who could see right through him. Her brown eyes sparked as she landed a hand on her hip. "Oh, you noticed."

Sam started to argue, then thought better of it. Dana was the kind of person who could sniff out a lie from three doors down. The marshals would have been better off tasking her as an interrogator than as an tech specialist.

Fact was, she'd only led him to say out loud what he'd already been thinking. Amy Brady was unlike any woman he'd ever met.

"You'll figure it out." As though dismissing him, Dana turned to her monitor and went to work, seeking intel in ways Sam could only sort of understand.

Sam nodded but didn't move. He needed to reset his expression and his thoughts before he headed up the hallway and into close proximity with Amy. She might be intriguing, but she was also his job. Crossing business with personal would make him hesitate in the clinch and could get them both killed. For him to do his job, he had to be focused, 100 percent on his game.

He stared at a monitor over Dana's head, the one tapped into the building's security cameras. Only a few people milled about, most of the nine-to-fivers in the other offices leaving for the day. No one appeared to be out of place, not that he'd expected anyone to be. Their location was a well-guarded secret.

"Be kind, Maldonado." Dana didn't turn from her work. "Feed her before she wastes away on that little pack of crackers."

Dana had to bring up those stupid crackers and remind him he had unfinished business with Amy. There was an interrupted conversation between them, a truth he had to tell before she could make decisions about her future. She had to know her sister was alive and well, at least for the moment. "Dana, can you do me a favor that makes you seem more like my secretary than a computer ninja?"

"Maybe. But it'll cost you dinner."

He smiled. "You've got it. Dinner's the next thing on my agenda." After he talked to Amy. His humor died quickly. "Call the police chief in Mountain Springs, North Carolina. Name's Arch Thompson. Make sure he knows we had to pick up Amy and that Jenna Clark might be in the crosshairs again. Have them bring her into protective custody if they feel the need to, but they have to let me know where she is if they do. Sooner or later, Amy could have the possibility of being reunited with her sister and—"

"My sister?"

Sam's breath caught in his throat. Across the room, Dana's hand froze on her track pad.

Letting out a ragged exhale, Sam closed his eyes and counted to five, the same way he'd done since he was a kid and had to face something he didn't want to. Maybe he'd imagined Amy's high strained voice. Maybe he was hungry or tired and this was all a horrible hallucination.

But footsteps behind him sliced off all hope. "Sam? What's this about my sister?"

He didn't turn toward her. Wasn't sure how he could face her when he'd been withholding information. The subterfuge had been necessary for both of their safety, but she wouldn't see it that way, not when he'd stepped down from his professional pedestal and crossed the line into friendship with her more than once, something he'd known all along he shouldn't do. "Where's Isaiah?"

"He took a phone call and stepped out of the room. I was looking for a restroom." Thinly veiled anger iced the words. "Now turn around, look me in the eye and tell me what's happened to my sister."

SEVEN

She'd heard him wrong. There was no way Sam had actually said what she believed she'd heard. Maybe fatigue had dulled her senses or brought on some sort of strange confusion. After all, Jenna Clark wasn't anyone she knew, let alone her sister.

But Sam had clearly said *Amy* and *reunited* and *her sister* in the same sentence.

Her knees weakened beneath her and Amy wobbled, reaching for the metal door frame as Sam turned to her, his expression guarded and closed in a way she'd never seen before, even when he was at his most professional. "Amy…"

"My sister is alive? And well?"

There was a slight hesitation, and Sam glanced over his shoulder at Dana.

Dana never turned away from the monitor she was intently studying, a series of progress bars flowing across the screen in multiple colors that seemed to bleed together. The multiple patterns made Amy's eyes twitch.

"Jenna is fine." Sam's voice dragged her attention to him.

There was that name again. Jenna. Amy's heart, which had started beating faster at the possibility of finally having information about her twin, seemed to thump harder against her rib cage.

He was wrong. Whoever he was talking about wasn't her sister. "I don't know anyone named Jenna. My sister is Eve. Her name is…" *Wait.* Amy's jaw slackened as the pieces fell into place. Jenna. Eve. "Genevieve. My sister's name is Genevieve." With her mother's penchant for the overly romantic, she'd saddled her twin daughters with names fit for any fairy-tale princess. Genevieve and Amaryllis. Amy's fingers went for the necklace she no longer wore, the delicate amaryllis pendant her sister had given to her years ago, the one Anthony had asked her to surrender to him before Amy Brady "died" in a horrific single-car accident in downtown El Paso.

She'd legally changed her name years ago, hating Amaryllis and all it represented about her past. Eve had held tight to her nickname while keeping her legal name, no matter how hard Amy had campaigned for her to change it.

Amy let her eyes slide closed and her chin drop to her chest, enjoying a prayer of thanks and a brief moment of blessed relief. Her sister was safe. She'd escaped Logan's clutches. Amy could stop waking up in the middle of the night tortured by visions of her twin sister's horrible death.

But it changed nothing. They could never be a family again, not only because WITSEC likely wouldn't allow it unless both of them were willing to go into hiding, but because there was no way what Amy had done when she'd introduced her sister to Logan Cutter would ever be forgivable. Amy might only be three minutes older, but she'd always been the responsible one, the one who made sure they were both fed and in school when their mother was off with her latest man. She'd always been the mother figure, the protector, yet when it mattered the most, she'd failed.

After letting the peace come to rest in a permanent place behind her heart, Amy opened her eyes to find Sam watching her.

He hadn't reached for her or touched her, but he leaned toward her slightly as though something in him wanted to.

But no. Amy wouldn't let him. He'd lied to her. She wouldn't let him comfort her in the aftermath. "So she changed her name from Eve to Jenna." It would be hard to shift her thinking. Much like herself, *Eve* had become an entirely different person. She'd become a *Jenna*.

Sam nodded, tight-lipped and grave. "After her last…" He inhaled deeply and searched the ceiling as though the words he needed might be written there in neon ink. "After her last altercation with Logan Cutter landed her in the hospital, Anthony Reynolds helped her escape. With our help, he changed her identity and got her a new start." The story ended abruptly, and Sam seemed to straighten and square his shoulders, almost as though he were daring her to ask more.

"She's okay?" Amy clinched her fists at her side to stop the shaking that had built from the inside out, threatening to rattle her into pieces. It was a tough fight to keep her teeth from knocking together. The emotion wasn't one she could pinpoint. Not fear. Not dread. Not even joy. This tidal wave defied description, rocking her core and heating her skin as though she had been hit with a sudden deathly fever.

"Last intel I had, yes." He tilted his head toward Dana. "As you heard, Dana is going to check in and make sure she's safe now."

"Why wouldn't she be?" Amy's words were heavy with a suspicion she wasn't even trying to hold back. Every ounce of the indefinable emotion overwhelming her drove into the question. There was more to this. Sam's posture, his demeanor, his tone of voice... All of it said he was hiding something else.

Sam stopped fidgeting and looked her square in the eye, his brown-eyed gaze unwavering. "Jenna is your *twin* sister. Other than you being a blonde and Jenna being a redhead, you're exactly the same. Until we know who's hunting for you, we have to assume they could mistake her for you. I'd rather operate with an abundance of caution than to keep my mouth shut, then wake up in the morning and find out your sister—" As Dana cleared her throat a little too loudly, Sam clamped his mouth shut and nodded. "I'd rather be safe than sorry."

So would Amy, for more reasons than Sam would ever know. "Does she know I'm alive?"

"You're in WITSEC. No one should know you're alive."

"Let's keep it that way." Amy pivoted on one heel and walked away, her hands still fisted, her stomach roiling around the crackers she'd washed down with a little too much water. Her sister was alive. She was safe.

And Anthony had known the whole time.

This heat sweeping through her was either intense anger or bone-rattling fear. Anger with Anthony for his extended silence. Fury with Sam for knowing the truth and not telling her. Terror that one day Amy would cross paths with her sister and be forced to face the disappointment and pain she'd caused. That she'd have to look her twin in the eye—the one person in the world who had been her closest friend and confidant—and pay for what she'd done to her.

Amy had ruined her sister's life, had nearly gotten her killed. Eve, Jenna, whatever her name was now would hate her, and Amy never wanted to see that look in her sister's eye. She'd prefer to remain dead to her for the rest of her life.

* * *

"Well, that went well." Dana's voice was low, full of a compassion that made Sam wince.

He'd almost rather she'd gone for full-blown derision or sarcasm. He deserved it. Sometimes, it was as though his team watched him flame out in disastrous failure and somehow missed the carnage for all of the smoke. Surely, Dana saw where he'd royally burned out in that entire encounter with Amy.

Dana could argue that Sam had done what the job dictated, and he shouldn't feel as though he'd wounded Amy. It wouldn't make a difference. Guilt dug into his shoulders with razor claws. If only he had told Amy about her sister when she brought the situation up in the car earlier. If only there had been two extra minutes with her in the other room before Isaiah had interrupted them. He could have told her himself, without her having to overhear. The fallout might have been hot, but it wouldn't have been nuclear.

The pain that had bled into Amy's expression had nearly compelled Sam to reach for her and pull her to him, in front of Dana and whomever else on the team decided to walk into the room.

Doing so would definitely have violated every protocol he could imagine.

"Go talk to her, Maldonado." Dana wasn't finished with him yet. "Don't let her wander off and stew over this. The longer she's angry, the angrier she'll get. She needs to understand why you couldn't tell her before now."

Maybe. Or maybe he should just walk up the hallway, knock on Watkins's door and turn Amy over to someone else entirely. He was definitely too personally invested.

Sam stood in the doorway. To the left was the room where Amy had retreated, the door tightly closed in a silent message of betrayal and anger. To the right was Watkins's office and the freedom forever from the responsibility for Amy Brady's life.

"I can practically read your thoughts from here." Dana walked up behind him and leaned over his shoulder. "Go to her. Don't abandon her on top of everything else. You're the only friend she has right now."

"I shouldn't be." Sam stepped into the hall, away from the weight of Dana's convictions. "Being a friend to her is the exact reason I should walk away."

"Sometimes it's more about people than it is about protocol." Dana planted her hands on his shoulders and turned him to the left. "It's okay to care about a person. To think of them as more than a case number. Go make sure she's okay. And then, if you care at all about any of us, you'll find some dinner somewhere."

Sam chuckled and walked up the hall to Amy's temporary quarters, his footfalls muffled by the carpet. With every step, his heart changed its mind, whiplashing between dread and anticipation. At the door, he hesitated and glanced toward Watkins's office, but Dana stood watching him. She gave him a gentle nod, then ducked out of sight.

Fine. He'd talk to Amy, or he'd never hear the end of it. Squaring his shoulders, Sam pulled his head from one side to the other to fight off some of the tension, then he tapped on Amy's door.

A muffled "What do you want?" was his only answer.

So she knew it was him. He eased the door open and slipped inside, leaving it cracked behind him. Some protocols shouldn't be violated, like being behind closed doors with a woman who made him feel things he really shouldn't feel on a mission...or ever.

Amy sat on the edge of the cot, her head in her hands. Far from angry, she appeared to be defeated, as though the knowledge of her sister's survival had added weight to her emotions instead of lifting a burden.

Sam eased down beside her, careful not to let his shoulder or elbow brush hers. "I'm sorry I didn't tell you sooner. I know it would have taken a lot of worry away if I had."

"You did your job."

Sam lifted an eyebrow. Well, that was unexpected.

Amy straightened and stared at the wall in front of her, unshed tears shining in her eyes and a haunted expression on her face. "How is she? Jenna?" The name came out awkwardly, as though she'd hesitated before choosing it over the *Eve* she was used to.

That question was a loaded cannon. Jenna had been through a lot in the past few months. It was because Grant Meyer had mistaken Jenna for Amy that the man had been arrested. But with the load Amy was apparently carrying right now, it wasn't the time to tell her all of the details. "She's fine. Engaged to a police officer."

"Really?" The news seemed to lift Amy's spirits a bit. "That's better than your sister tying you to a human trafficker."

Sam didn't know what to say. The depths of Amy's pain were deeper than he was qualified to plumb. While his own heart felt the razor's cuts of the hurt, his mind couldn't wrap around why she was feeling it. Somehow, based on her comment, she felt some responsibility for what Cutter had done to Jenna, but the burden wasn't hers and should never have been hers.

Logan Cutter and Grant Meyer were scum. They preyed on the weak and valued their pockets over any sort of human decency or dignity. None of what they'd done was Amy's fault. "You can't blame yourself."

Hmm. Seemed he'd heard Dana say the same to him. Sam shoved her voice aside. This was a completely different situation.

"Don't do that." Amy jerked her head toward him, a certain fire in her eyes that said she was angry after all, and she was about to unleash the full force of her fury on him. "Don't talk about things when you have no idea what you're talking about."

"Why don't you tell me?"

One tear broke free and blazed a trail down

her cheek, then another followed. "I can't." Her voice broke. "You'll look at me differently." She turned away, leaving Sam with a clear view of the back of her head.

And her fist around his heart.

Sam gave up. There was no pretending he didn't feel differently about—feel more for—Amy than he had any other witness he'd ever worked with. She was his friend and he was hers. Dana was right about their relationship, and pretending the situation was different would only end up hurting them both.

"Come here." Sam reached for Amy. He had to hold her, touch her, let her know she wasn't in this alone and someone cared.

Her body stiffened, and she resisted for a second, but as he reached around her waist and pulled her closer, her muscles seemed to give up and she sank against him, turning her face into his chest. There were no tears, no shaking shoulders. Just a silent surrender, a contentment to let Sam bear a part of her burden, if only for a moment.

Wrapping his arms around her, Sam rested his chin on her head, breathing in the clean scent of whatever her shampoo was, her hair soft on his skin. Man, she really was stronger than anyone else he'd ever met. Stronger and more honest, more vulnerable and more loyal...

She was everything Lindsay had never been.

The thought ripped through him, tightening his arms around Amy as it nearly strangled him. No. No way. It was one thing to think of Amy as a friend, another entirely to compare her to his ex-wife.

Amy pulled away slightly and lifted her head. She must have felt the shift in his demeanor, might even have been close enough to read the thought as it rocketed across his mind.

Her eyebrows drew together as she searched his expression, trying to read what he was thinking.

And what he was thinking was she was too close. Not just in proximity but too close to his heart. His heart...which was beating about ten times too fast in his chest, loud enough for her to hear it in the silence, he was certain.

He wanted to back away. Wanted to put space between them, but he couldn't. Her gravity was greater than his strength to resist.

Dana was wrong. Sam couldn't be Amy's friend. He was too far past simple friendship. At some point during all of those meetings with Amy and Edgecombe, she'd made her way into his heart. Her face had become the face he saw in those rare moments he dared to dream of a future wife, home and family. This was the reason she'd seemed so overly familiar earlier, because she lived in his head, whether he wanted her to or not.

The air between them shifted and he kept watching her eyes; he could see the exact moment his thoughts were mirrored in hers, the exact moment a type of wonder softened her expression and her eyes dropped to his lips.

Pulling her closer, Sam granted the request she hadn't voiced, brushing his lips against hers softly, then responding as she met him in the kiss.

His eyes drifted shut and the rest of the world faded into nothing. No danger. No job. No nothing outside of Amy Brady and the peace her kiss brought to his heart.

EIGHT

Sam Maldonado was kissing her.

She was kissing Sam Maldonado.

Amy threaded her arms around his neck and lost herself in a moment she prayed would never end. He'd haunted her dreams almost from the moment she first laid eyes on him. He'd had her heart skipping twice every time he'd shown up at her apartment with Deputy Edgecombe.

And she'd denied it as though her life depended on it. Maybe it did, because he was only doing his job. But as the moment drew longer, Amy didn't care to think any longer. She only cared that, for the first time in three years—maybe longer—she felt as though she knew who she was and where she belonged.

She felt as though she'd finally found a home.

Had felt that way almost from the moment

Sam had found her mired in her own foolishness when she'd fled WITSEC to search for Layla and he'd rescued her.

He'd rescued her.

With a gasp, Amy broke away, shoving Sam in the chest and stumbling to her feet. She stared down at him, still able to feel his lips on hers, her heart screaming that she was doing the wrong thing while her head argued with a ferocity she couldn't deny.

Sam had been her rescuer. Twice. She was no better than her mother, falling for the fairy tale of the knight in shining armor. Her hands went to her mouth, pressing her lips, trying to destroy the sensation of his kiss. Maybe if she could make that go away, she could forget the way he made her heart feel.

Like she really was alive and ready to do more than hide for the rest of her life.

Sam was on his feet almost as fast as she was, regret written all over his expression in a way she could almost read. "Amy. I never should have…" He dragged his hands down his face, almost as though he too was trying to scrub away the moment forever. "That was wrong." Sliding his hand to the back of his neck, he walked to the door and stood staring through the crack, kneading muscles in his neck.

Amy dropped her gaze to the floor. She knew why she'd backed away, but he didn't have to regret it as well. Her heart ached at the implied rejection. She was a job. A moment. An irrational action.

Nothing more. And she would never be anything more.

She could never let him know he'd wounded her. Pulling herself to her full height, she crossed her arms over her stomach and stared at the back of his head. "Forget it. It was nothing. A lot's happened today. We're both tired and we've both been through a lot. That's the only thing that happened here. Nothing more."

Sam flinched, then froze, almost as though her words had hit him with a kidney punch. When he turned to face her, his expression was stone. "You're right. We can just forget it and move on from here."

He'd never been so cold, so professional with her. Amy fought hard to keep the pain from leaking out of her eyes.

Jerking his thumb over his shoulder, Sam said, "In fact, I should walk up the hall right now and let Deputy Watkins know you need someone else to care for you. He can task Isaiah with—"

"No." The word ripped out before Amy could stop it, an involuntary reaction to the thought of losing him. Sam might be unattainable, and his presence might be breaking her heart, but he was all she had, the only person in the world she trusted. If he left her alone… "Please."

She hated herself. Hated the pleading in her voice, the reminder that she was no better than her mother and, in fact, might be infinitely worse. But she needed Sam. No one else made her feel safe. "You're the only one who knows what to do if I panic again." It was lame, but it was all she had short of begging him not to leave, and she would never sink so low.

"I don't know if this is such a good idea."

She was losing him. There had to be a way… "Layla. I'm the only one who can help you reach out to Layla. She won't let you near her otherwise. Sam, if you're going to save her, you need me."

He eyed her for a long moment as though he could see the desperation in her suggestion and wanted to tell her no. Finally, he looked away from her, out the door, away from the friendship they'd ruined when they kissed. "I think the best thing to do is—"

"Sam!" Another voice overlapped his, rocketing up the hallway with an urgency that snapped the thread between them as footsteps pounded closer. Isaiah shoved past Sam into the room and cast a frantic glance at Amy. His gun was drawn and held low at his side as he pushed the door open wider and faced Sam, shoving a backpack into his hand. "Both of you have to move now. Get her out of here. The building has been compromised."

Sam slung the backpack over his shoulder. A go-bag packed with essentials for survival, everything from spare clothing to a prepaid debit card to a burner cell phone. Isaiah handing it over only meant one thing.

They were in deep trouble.

His mind spun through too many questions, too fast. Who'd found them? How could he get Amy out? How was he supposed to protect her when she'd scrambled his emotions and his mind into mush? He turned to Amy. "Put on your vest." He still wore his beneath his shirt, too warm to be comfortable.

Isaiah stepped into the hallway and looked both ways before heading out the door. "Get her out of here. Watkins is already with Traynor and Barclay clearing a path for you down the stairwell. Don't tell me where you're headed but get moving. Don't make any contact with anyone here until Watkins contacts you."

Sam's sidearm was in his hand and he'd laced his fingers with Amy's, dragging her toward the front of the office behind Isaiah. "What's going on?"

Amy clung to him, silent, though her face had paled to the point Sam feared he might have to throw her over his shoulders and carry her out of the building. He wanted to squeeze her hand and tell her it was going to be okay, but he couldn't. He had no idea what was going on.

Isaiah kept pace beside him. "Dana found how deep they accessed Edgecombe's computer. Deep enough to know about this place and to post the location on the dark web. His phone was tapped too, and until ours can be checked, every device we have is suspect. Looks like we're outed to anyone who wants to come looking for us. And the red car that was following you earlier today? It just pulled into the parking garage. No telling if he's alone, the first wave or the last piece someone is setting into place. They're already moving against us."

Sam pulled his phone from his pocket and dropped it on the cot. Someone knew they were here. While the team could likely deal with one assailant in that car, there were no telling how many others there were or how many would come behind him if the building was compromised. "Who's breaking down the office?" There were protocols in place, and securing their intel was priority number one.

"Dana's already started the process. We've got this. The office isn't your concern. You get Amy out of here. And you're dark until further notice. No contact means no way they can track you."

Great. It was him in the wind with Amy, no backup. He understood the protocol in a situation as desperate as this one. Around the country, other agents were likely going on high alert, taking precautions they'd never dreamed they'd have to take. Sam didn't want to think how far this would ripple.

He'd have to worry about that later. Isaiah was already headed out the door. "I'll take the stairs ahead of you and make sure it's clear. Dana's keeping eyes on the camera monitors and is going to be our eyes in front and behind." He stopped Sam at the door into the main hall and pressed a set of keys into Sam's hand. "Take my truck. It's my personal vehicle. Nobody will know to track that. Give me a twenty-count head start, then go down the stairs."

Sam started to grab Isaiah by the wrist and tell him they needed to switch places, that he wasn't fit to be Amy's protector anymore. But he hesitated too long, and Isaiah slipped out the glass-fronted door into the hall.

He couldn't leave Amy behind anyway. He needed to know she was safe, and as much as he lacked faith in himself, he wasn't sure whom else he could truly trust with their world burning down around them.

Sam started the count in his head, fighting his mind's urge to start at forty-two.

Twenty. Isaiah had said twenty. If he focused on one thing at a time, doing what his team expected of him and following procedure, Amy would be safe.

She had to be.

Sam prayed Isaiah was counting at the same speed he was. For all tactical purposes, he was deaf, his earpiece abandoned on the desk in his office. There was no time to go get it now. He'd have to trust his senses.

Sam drew Amy close behind him, their hands sandwiched against his back. She dropped her head to his shoulder blade, her breathing ragged, her forehead warm through his shirt.

Squeezing her fingers, he shoved his feelings for her aside and shifted into a cold mental game as he steeled himself to move. "I'm going to get you out of this. I promise."

He shouldn't make promises he had no idea if he could keep, but Sam steadied his nerves and prepared for flight. There was no way he was going to fail this time. The current danger was his fault for letting his guard down by sinking into his emotions.

He couldn't let Amy Brady pay for his mistakes with her life.

NINE

The world was moving too fast. Amy was numb, unsure whether this was real or if her mind had broken up with reality.

She wanted to lock herself into the room where she'd been with Sam, but even that was devastating after the kiss and rejection. Still, it had to be safer behind closed doors than it was in front of a glass door with only Sam and his drawn pistol between her and death.

Trust me.

He'd said those words in the car and she'd embraced them as though they could save her. Sam had crushed her heart, but he was the only hope she had to keep her heart beating another day.

His fingers tightened around hers—hands that had already protected her, had already proven capable at keeping her safe. He was preparing to run.

In that moment, there was no doubt. Amy would follow Sam wherever he led. He was the only safety she had in this rapidly shifting world. Well, Sam and God, and she was starting to wonder if the thing in Psalm 139 about God having her days written down was a giant lie.

"Let's go." Before she was ready, Sam shoved the door open and tugged Amy behind him. They raced up the main hallway past the elevator to the stairs.

Nine flights of stairs. Amy's knees quaked, fear and adrenaline overriding exhaustion and hunger. Her knees couldn't hold up for that many flights down. As Sam burst through the fire door, it was clear she had no choice. She'd have to find reserves.

At each landing he paused, his head tilted as he listened for sounds below them. In the metal and concrete stairwell, every breath echoed, every footstep thundered.

When they reached the bottom, her legs were shaking, liquefied by fear and exertion. Her heart pounded, and dangerous black spots danced before her eyes as her lungs worked triple-time. She needed a second to pull it together so she wouldn't drop like a dead woman.

The thought of Sam having to peel her off the floor drove her on. She couldn't be the weak one who proved to be an inconvenience once again.

Isaiah was waiting for them by a heavy metal fire door at the rear of the building. "My truck's six meters to your left. Nobody's out there but you need to move fast. I'll go ahead and cover you."

Dropping her forehead to the back of Sam's shoulder, Amy fought for breath and prayed Isaiah wouldn't be another casualty in the fight for her life. *Lord, please. Don't let anyone else die because of me. Please.*

They were moving before she was ready, across the lot and into the cab of a pickup truck before she could process.

This was too fast. Too much. Amy grabbed the handle above the door as Sam shifted the truck into Reverse and pressed the gas. She needed information, something to orient her mind and to provide some control. If she knew where they were heading, that there was a plan she could wrap her head around, she might be able to fight off the panic attack that was already turning her stomach into jelly. "Where are we going?"

"We have a safe house in the mountains a couple of hours away."

Two hours on the road in full view of the entire world? Fear danced across Amy's shoulders, pounding tension into a headache that ran up the back of her neck and into her temples. She hadn't had to flee to a safe house since the very first night when her life had changed forever.

"Somebody managed to to clone Edgecombe's laptop and locate our headquarters. I have to keep you out of sight as best as I can on my own until Dana can figure out how much the hacker accessed and if they're on the inside."

Amy dug her fingers into her knees, trying to hold on. She'd already had two panic attacks today. She definitely didn't want to battle a third. "That can't be."

"Looks like it is."

"How do you know they can't locate your safe house? Isn't that in your database?"

Adjusting the heat in the vehicle, Sam shook his head. "Most of our safe houses aren't documented."

Well, that was one thing in her favor, she guessed. One out of a thousand conspiring against her.

They rode in silence, Amy playing the childhood games with road signs until those thinned out. She'd do anything to keep her mind from running away with her.

She didn't know how long they'd been on the road when Sam finally spoke. "You hungry at all?"

Adrenaline and the fact they were already winding upward into the mountains in the dark probably wouldn't let her handle food. "You can stop if you need to, but I'm good."

"I'll be okay." He probably would. Sam seemed to be the kind of guy who could go days without food or sleep or anything else normal human beings needed to survive.

Amy turned her head and watched the trees, which were taller now that they'd made it into the foothills. If her geography was correct, they shouldn't be too far from Toccoa, where Anthony told her he had sent Layla.

Straightening in her seat, Amy watched the road. Maybe she could talk Sam into finding Layla. Or maybe she'd have the opportunity to slip away and reach Layla on her own. When she did, she'd have to be more methodical than the last time. Sam had found her quickly a few months ago when she'd headed out on her own.

She worked her jaw from side to side, trying to relieve the pressure in her ears as the altitude increased.

"Look, Amy—" he yawned, apparently suffering the same ear pressure issues as Amy was "—I don't know what whoever killed Meyer is capable of. I know you're thinking of taking off on your own to find Layla, but—"

"What?" *Great.* Now he could read her mind.

"Don't act surprised." As they straightened out of a curve, Sam turned onto a different road and the truck climbed gently again. "Whoever killed Meyer has reach. Until we know who that is, you're in danger, even if Meyer is dead."

"Maybe they don't want me now that he's gone."

"If that's the case, who's chasing you?" He navigated a hairpin turn. "You're still in serious danger."

"You think I don't know that?"

"Yeah, I think you're purposely ignoring that fact."

Wow. Her skin bristled, anger once again amping up enough to shove fear aside. "I'm sorry? What are you trying to say?"

"Three months ago, you broke the rules when you ran off on your own without protection on some half-baked rescue mission, all while you knew Meyer was out to find you."

"And?"

"And you're still trying to think of a way to get to Layla." When her shoulders dropped, he acted as though he had more to say but seemed to change gears. "This isn't something to be flippant about. Trust me enough to help you and Layla. Trust me enough to keep you safe. WITSEC hasn't failed you so far, even if you did go off the radar on us."

He had no idea what she'd been through, no idea why she'd made the decisions she had and why she'd continue to make those same decisions. Deputy Marshal Samuel Maldonado had no right to judge her. "You haven't failed me? Aren't we running away from your very safe super-secret headquarters because someone breached your data system?"

He winced and was wise enough not to reply.

"I can take care of myself."

"What would you have done if my team and I hadn't been there today? Hit that dude with your monster attitude?"

Wow. Okay then. So he was a bigger jerk

than she'd initially thought. Apparently, kissing him had been an even bigger mistake than she'd realized. "I'd have…" *Probably lost my life.* The fight in Amy died. If he hadn't arrived at the school, she'd be dead. There was no way around it. "You're right."

His eyebrows rose. "Wow. Wasn't expecting that."

"Well then, here's another surprise. I'm sorry." She was. She'd let her fear at the situation and disappointment at his rejection burn into anger and unleashed her out-of-control emotions on him. He didn't deserve it. He was doing his job and doing it well.

"Thank you." At least he accepted her apology with some grace.

He was right about something else too— not that she was ready to tell him. He was the one thing she had going for her. The only choice she had in the middle of this dark, terrifying night was to trust the man determined to be her knight in shining armor.

No one had ever wanted to be her rescuer.

It felt right. She wrapped her arms around her stomach. *Right* was something she shouldn't feel, especially not about a man who was only interested in rescuing her because it was how he earned his paycheck, no matter that he'd kissed her only an hour or so earlier.

His demeanor after had said everything she needed to know. Amy was a box to check off. Nothing more. She'd do well to remember her place in his life. "How far is this safe house?"

"You let me handle the driving. Trust me and try to relax."

They rode in silence and had wound down into a valley before Amy cracked. She couldn't bear the stillness any longer. "You used to be a soldier?" The question came out of nowhere, though the thought had tweaked the back of her mind earlier. There was the mention of knowing the Arghandab Valley. The way he'd walked the road, watching. Something about his measured movements, the slight swagger, the way he held his posture was entirely too familiar. The army trained a certain *something* into its men and women, a *something* that set them apart from civilians. She'd seen it in El Paso in the guys stationed at Fort Bliss. She'd seen it in Noah during the brief time they'd had together before he was killed.

A muscle ticked in Sam's jaw, barely visible in the faint bluish light from the dash, but the movement was there nonetheless. "I was."

"And now?"

"Now I'm not."

Now I'm not. The words reached across the space between them and wrapped around her heart, finding a companion in her own brokenness. *Now I'm not.*

Amy was no longer a lot of things. No longer a personal trainer working her way through college and a doctorate in sports medicine. No longer a long list of past accomplishments. No longer a twin sister.

And as of this afternoon, no longer an adjunct professor. No longer a friend to the small circle of companions she'd had in Georgia. No longer Amy Brady. No longer Amy Naylor.

Ever since the federal marshals had packed her up and moved her out of El Paso, faked her death and dropped a new identity over her like an ill-fitting pair of hand-me-down blue jeans, she'd had no idea who she was, where she fit in or what was even reality. If she wasn't Amy Brady, who was she? What made Amy Naylor tick? Now, she was about to go through the whole process again. It was more than one person could handle. "I feel that right along with you," she muttered as Sam slowed the truck and turned onto a bumpy dirt road that ought to scare the horror movie lover in her right into a heart attack.

As a small cabin came into view in the headlights, Amy turned toward Sam. "Hey, thank you for this. I don't know what—"

The driver's side mirror shattered. Sam slammed the truck to a halt as the echo of a gunshot cracked across the clearing.

"Get down!" Sam shifted the truck into Reverse, then reached over and shoved the back of Amy's head toward her knees. There was no way the truck's doors would stop a heavy-duty bullet if it found its way between the mechanisms inside, but thin sheet metal was a whole lot safer than glass windows.

Amy said nothing, simply obeyed as she dug her head between her knees.

Sam hoped she was praying. Pressing the gas almost to the floor, he hung a J-turn, the truck's tires spinning for traction on a thick bed of leaves. As the front end swung around, another gunshot cracked and a bullet popped against metal. Whoever was firing wasn't a sharpshooter, but they only needed one good shot to make his night a whole lot worse.

Sam shifted into Drive and strained with the truck as it hesitated to move. Another gunshot, another *thwack*, this one louder, harsher. A sharp burn bit into the back of Sam's left leg. Swallowing the cry that wanted to escape, he prayed for forward motion as the truck's bed fishtailed before it gained traction. They shot forward way too fast, bouncing along the rutted drive toward the road. "You okay?" If the bullet that had clipped him had hit Amy…

"Fine." Her voice rattled with the jolt as the truck bottomed out in a rut. "You?"

"Fine. Stay down until I know we're clear." His relief at Amy's safety was short-lived. He had to put distance between them and the cabin fast, before the shooter could pursue.

The truck careened onto the road, engine screaming as Sam pushed it to its limits, headed north and deeper into the mountainside forest.

It was hopefully the last direction the shooter would expect them to be heading. Help was behind them, toward Atlanta. In front of them? Sam scrolled through possibilities. They were slim. He'd only used this safe house one other time, with Devin Wallace, so either their safe houses were compromised or someone knew where Sam had been headed.

Without his team, Sam was on his own.

This wasn't his wheelhouse. He didn't do long-term protection details, not since Wallace. No one was ever in his care long enough for Sam to lose them.

This situation called for an entirely different kind of plan, but there were too many things vying for attention in his brain, and they all circled back to one undeniable question.

Who was behind this? The Marshals Service prided itself on the integrity and skill of its people, especially in WITSEC and particularly on elite teams like Sam's. No one in the program who'd followed the rules had ever been harmed. The idea that there was a mole in WITSEC was ludicrous. This had to be from the outside, from the hack of Edgecombe's laptop.

He checked the rearview and saw no lights behind them. In darkness this deep, following them without headlights would be suicide. For the moment, they were clear. "You can sit up. I'd hate for you to get car sick."

Amy eased upright, her face pale in the dim light.

Lord, please don't let her panic again. They couldn't stop. It was too risky. He had to get her off the road, somewhere safe where they could regroup and he could make a plan that didn't involve constant change on the fly. He reached down and felt his calf, where the bullet had grazed. His jeans were intact, which meant the bullet hadn't drawn blood. "You okay?"

"If you're asking if I was hit, I'm fine. Whether or not I'm *okay* is up for debate."

"You'll feel better after I find you a safe place to rest." With events piling up, there was no way Amy could hold it together for long. Sam needed rest as well if he was going to keep going solo.

"I can't remember the last time I rested."

Sam could relate. She was talking about much more than the past day. Her life had been a whirlwind for three years, looking over her shoulder and wondering when the hit would come.

His life had been a series of bad choices and mistakes that got other people hurt. The fact he hadn't lost a witness since Devin Wallace had to be a fluke.

"Sam?"

He jerked into the present, the hum of the tires and the tension radiating off Amy snapping his thoughts into clarity. Her voice was stretched thin, as though she fought for breath. Her fingers dug into the seat.

He knew that feeling as well. She was riding the edge of another panic attack.

Sam reached across and lifted her hand from the seat. He wrapped his fingers around hers and held on. Human contact. Amy needed to know she wasn't alone. He was here for her. "What can I do to help?"

"Talk to me. About anything. About…" She pulled in a shuddering breath. "About you."

Sam looked away from her and out the windshield. He'd almost missed a bend in the road. See? He wasn't the one who should be protecting her. Someone who wouldn't get distracted by whatever current ran between them should be in the driver's seat.

But there was no other option. "What do you want to know?"

"Whatever you'll tell but make it interesting." She straightened, turning her hand so her fingers laced with his. "Are you married?"

Sam snorted. "Why? You interested?" *Keep it light, Maldonado.* Although he should have kicked himself for the joke. It sounded as though he were making light of their earlier kiss. And it certainly hadn't been *light* to him.

"No." She tilted her head, oblivious to his disappointment at the quickness of her answer. "Seems like a good story."

"I'm not married."

"You're not? Or you tell people that because your job is intense, and you don't want people knowing about your family?"

Normally, he'd fall back on a cover. He already had a backstory ready so he wouldn't have to share personal information. Tonight, his brain was too fried, and Amy was too... Amy. He opened his mouth and the truth poured out. "I'm not married anymore."

"You used to be?"

"When I was in the army. It was a long time ago."

"What happened?"

Sam stared out the windshield, the two-lane mountain road passing through a series of turns as they leveled out into a valley. He'd only talked to one other person about Lindsay.

He'd never told anyone he'd suffered with panic attacks... At least, not until he'd told Amy tonight.

It really didn't matter what he said. Soon,

he'd pass her over to a team that would oversee her relocation and he'd never see her again. The pressure to speak built in his chest. It would be a release to tell someone the truth. "Let's just say Lindsay's strength wasn't being faithful."

Amy sucked air between her teeth. She squeezed his fingers, then relaxed her hold. It seemed she'd forgotten she was touching him at all.

That was okay with Sam. It was pretty rare he had human contact, and hers was different. Somehow, it seemed to make the pain that usually came with speaking Lindsay's name a little less sharp. "In the army, I was on a team that was gone more than it was home, and she tended to use my time away to do her own thing."

"That was a seminice way to say a very ugly thing."

Sam kneaded the steering wheel. "Maybe."

"You knew?"

His jaw clinched. Extracting his hand from Amy's, Sam moved it to his knee. This was why he never talked about the implosion of his marriage. In the end, he looked foolish, and the truth about his emotional inadequacies was revealed.

He hadn't been enough for his wife. Over and over, she'd accused him of being emotionless. Over and over, he'd refused to change. He'd told himself she didn't understand the stresses of being a soldier in a post-9/11 world. She didn't understand his need to hide inside himself or to go out with his team in order to forget.

None of his actions would excuse hers, but he'd provided the reasons she'd needed to stray. He'd failed to be there for her, therefore, his marriage had failed. Not only that, but he'd been the idiot who kept coming home to her, even after he knew what she'd done.

It had taken the divorce papers to shock him into reality and to knock the bottle out of his hand. He hadn't touched anything stronger than root beer since the day the judge signed off. It was too little, too late. So Sam had left the military and joined the US Marshals, determined to save others when he couldn't save himself.

Even there, he'd failed.

"I can practically read your mind from here." Amy leaned against the door so she could turn toward him. "You blame yourself."

Sam concentrated on a series of S-curves. He'd said too much. She seemed to have relaxed and eased away from the ledge of fear, so they could change the subject any time.

"You shouldn't," she said.

"No? You were there? You know all of the thoughts in my head?" Who was she to tell him how to feel, who he was? He was a joke. A nobody. A monumental failure at even the most basic relationships. "I kept taking her back."

"She was your touchstone, the best chance you had at stability in a world out of control. If you were on a team, I'm guessing you served with Special Forces or something deeper. Your job was intense. You saw things, maybe even did things, that kept you awake at night. You needed the dream of her. You needed to believe this time would be different. When you were slogging through garbage overseas, the dream of a picket-fence life was the thing that kept you going."

The woman sounded like a psychology textbook. *Wait a second...* Sam winced. He was a triple idiot. "This is what I get for telling my secrets to a psychology minor."

"You should have known better." She toyed with the hem of her shirt, pulling it between her fingers, seeming to lose some of her confidence. "Am I right?"

Sam pulled his eyes from her and back to the road for the hundredth time. He had to stop letting her distract him. Lights softened the horizon, and he aimed the truck toward them.

Was she right? He'd never thought of it that way. He'd always assumed he was the sap, the punch line to Lindsay's jokes, even if his dismissal of her emotions was terrible. "I don't know. When you put it that way, you make it sound like I used her."

"No, you had an expectation. It was probably born out of your childhood. Either your parents had an ideal marriage and you were striving for the same, or your home life was a wreck and you were trying to do the opposite of…" She trailed off and turned in the seat, facing out the windshield. "Never mind. None of this is my business, and I shouldn't have said anything. I'm sorry."

She didn't have to apologize. She'd given him a release he hadn't realized he needed. He'd popped the cork on his memories, had told someone the truth and the pain had eased into a dull ache. "Don't say you're sorry. I chose to talk about it." Although he was stopping the conversation now. Delving into his childhood wasn't a trip he was willing to take.

Besides, this was supposed to be about Amy and backing her away from another panic attack. "Are you feeling better now?"

"Surprisingly, yes."

Sam exhaled the breath he hadn't realized he'd been holding as he turned onto an interstate and hopefully toward a hotel. Thankfully, his go-bag held a prepaid card that would get them whatever they needed. Right now, that big need was rest, though he doubted sleep would come to either of them as long as a killer was on their trail.

TEN

With her back to the mirror in the hotel's bathroom, Amy stretched out her arm and examined the material of her royal blue button-down shirt. There was dirt on the arm, probably from where she'd slid down the side of Sam's car earlier.

Too bad. It was her favorite shirt, one she'd bought not long after she'd become Amy Naylor. In her old life, she'd have never worn something so dressy, would have lived in athletic clothes and polos. Yet another difference between her real self and this dressed-up role she played.

This morning, when she'd chosen this shirt from her closet in preparation for yet another day in her WITSEC-created career as a biology professor, felt like a lifetime ago.

In a way, it probably was, since the life she'd lived and the person she'd been when she pulled this shirt from the hanger this morning no longer existed.

She wrinkled her nose and finger-combed her blond hair, avoiding the steam-covered mirror. If she could help it, she kept away from mirrors as much as possible. The eyes that looked back knew too many things about her, things she wished they didn't know. The guilt always rushed in doubly hard when she had to look herself in the eye, so she typically gave her reflection a cursory glance to make sure her hair was in place, her makeup wasn't a mess and her clothes were hanging right. She never lingered.

Amy brushed dirt off the hip of her black pants, then gave up. They were going to stay dirty. It had probably been kind of pointless to take a shower since she'd had to climb into the same clothes she'd been wearing, but the hot water had eased some of the aches in her body and brought a quiet to her brain that might let her catch a nap before a nightmare shoved her into reality.

Or before she remembered Sam's kiss again. For one brief moment, she'd felt as though she knew who she was.

It was all a lie. Had that been the feeling her mother was searching for all of those years with all of those men? The feeling of being alive, of being her true self? Or had it been something completely different?

It didn't matter. No matter what Sam Maldonado made her feel, there were too many reasons to keep him at arm's length. She wouldn't become her mother. She was nothing more than his assignment. Soon, he'd disappear to help the next witness and she'd vanish into a new place, a new name, a new identity.

The thought made her nauseous.

Then again, she was starving and that wasn't helping her gut settle. She should have told Sam to hit a drive-through, but she hadn't been hungry when he asked and he'd been focused on finding a hotel far enough away from the interstate to throw anyone behind them off their trail. Surely, they were safe here. Surely, no one would follow them this far.

Oh, the lies she told herself.

Amy flipped the bathroom light switch and stepped into her room. The hum of the monster air-conditioning units beneath her window pulsed in the room, the kind of white noise that would either lull her to sleep or keep her awake, straining to hear over it.

She paused by the closed door that connected her small room with Sam's. No sound leaked through the door. Maybe he was getting some sleep. The door stood shut between them, but he'd insisted she keep her side unlocked in case she needed him.

What was Sam worried about? It wasn't like someone could break into her room without a keycard, and she'd secured every latch. They were on the second floor. She was as safe as she could get.

And that fact still probably wouldn't let her sleep.

The room glowed with the light from the bedside lamp, and on top of the bedspread lay a candy bar and a bottle of water. Amy whirled toward the door. Sam must have known she'd be starving and was doing the best he could to provide for her.

Sinking onto the edge of the bed, Amy ripped open the candy bar and ate two bites, staring at the swirls in the carpet's pattern. Deputy Marshal Sam Maldonado was the strangest man she'd ever met, closed off and by the book one minute, then totally wide-open and acting as though he were her best friend the next. Kissing her one minute, then vanishing into his job the next. He was very good at what he did, although he didn't seem to think so. There was a slight hesitation to his actions, almost as though he thought them through twice before he made the leap.

Something had happened to shake his confidence, something that had likely started in his childhood and been blown even farther into the stratosphere by his ex-wife's behavior. He'd acted as though Amy ought to fault him for staying with the woman when she was running around on him, but Amy could understand. Her own childhood had been a fragmented mess. She could sympathize with his need for stability.

There was something more though, a thread of self-doubt that had to do with his job even more than his personal life. For some reason, Sam Maldonado believed he would never be good enough.

Sort of like her. She could thank her mother for that insecurity though. Neither Amy nor her sister had been enough to keep their mother home. Their love hadn't measured up to what she needed.

Cracking open the water bottle, Amy washed down her meager meal, then propped herself up on the bed against the pillows, giving the pale beige wall a wry smile. Amaryllis and Genevieve. At least the years had given her enough distance so that she could smile about her name being a character in one of her mother's princess fairy-tale fantasies.

Amy rolled onto her side, pulling her knees to her chest and tucking her chin as she curled into the fetal position. When their mother had left them alone as children, she and Eve had climbed into her bed together, pressing their backs to one another. It was a defense mechanism; she knew that now. They'd had each other's backs, seeking comfort while facing whatever threat might come at them from the outside. They'd been so young, so scared, so brave. Eve had always seemed a little bit younger and Amy had been the one to take care of her, to comfort her when she was scared and to fend for them when they only had peanut butter and bread and crackers for survival.

Coffee was cheap though, and there were nights when the sisters had curled up with hot mugs, sitting on opposite ends of the couch, pretending they were all grown up and had oh-so-important things to discuss.

The memory clawed at her heart. They'd never had the chance to move their imaginings into reality. If Amy hadn't taken the job at New Horizons… If she'd realized sooner what Grant Meyer was up to… If she'd known the kind of man Logan Cutter was before she introduced him to her sister…

Maybe they'd still be each other's best friends and they'd still have each other's backs. Maybe Eve never would have been hurt, never would have cut Amy out of her life. Maybe neither of them would have had to flee El Paso in order to save their own lives.

Drawing herself into a tighter ball, Amy shut her eyes and tried to block out the memories. What good were they when she could never have her sister back again?

She blamed Amy for her pain. They could never be sisters again, and the best thing for Amy to do was to stay out of Eve's life forever.

Out of *Jenna's* life forever. The pain in her heart seeped into her body until her joints ached. Amy didn't even know her own sister's name anymore.

She drifted on that horrible, crushing thought, halfway between wakefulness and sleep until a soul-splitting cry, like an animal in pain, roared into her room.

Sam.

Amy was on her feet, running for their adjoining door. She pulled her side open and shoved on his. It was locked.

The cry came again, lower this time, the sound of movement drifting in with it. Violent movement.

Amy pounded on the door, then shrank away, twisting her fingers together. Sam was in trouble and she was helpless to save him.

Sam bent at the waist, hands braced on his knees, the rough feel of blue jeans against his palms all wrong. He should be wearing his army combat uniform and sweating under the Afghan sun. There should be explosions, the metallic scent of blood and the smoky residue of gunfire. There should be screams besides his own, which still echoed in his ears.

It had to have been a nightmare, because the visions were all wrong. Instead of one of his teammates lying bloodied on the ground before him, the lifeless eyes that stared up at him in the vision had belonged to Devin Wallace. The two bloodiest days of his life had merged into one horrible, toxic blend to remind him of the man he never was and never could be.

He heaved in air and tried to remember when he'd fallen asleep, where he'd fallen asleep. Tried to rid himself of a nightmare that had invaded all five of his senses and burrowed into his soul. All too real. All too filled with memories he'd give everything to forget. Wherever he was, it was dark and cool. Light filtered under a door.

His heart drummed so loudly he could hear it.

"Sam!"

That wasn't his heartbeat. Someone was pounding on a door. He straightened as the voice dragged him into the present. Amy. They were in adjoining hotel rooms in a small town between Toccoa, Georgia, and Asheville, North Carolina. As his eyes adjusted, the room came into focus. He was standing by the bed, fully clothed, dragged to his feet by the invasion of his mind.

He inhaled, let the breath settle and hoped his voice wouldn't crack when he spoke. "Everything's fine. It's okay."

But it wasn't. If he'd cried out loud enough to awaken her, then it wouldn't take her long to figure out his secret. She was smart, intuitive to the point he was almost afraid to think around her for fear she'd somehow read his mind.

Even worse, if she'd heard him, it was likely

someone else had, even though the hotel had appeared to be half empty when they arrived. What if someone came to check on them or, worse, called the police? There wasn't time for that kind of red tape, and that kind of attention drawn to them could end disastrously.

The pounding stopped. Maybe she'd taken his word for it and would get some rest. She probably needed it more than he did. He was used to being awake for long periods of time. He could handle it. Had been handling it for years.

Sinking to the edge of the bed, Sam snapped on the light and dragged his hands down his face, scrubbing against two days' worth of stubble. He'd lain down for a minute to get some quick shut-eye while the shower ran in Amy's room and he must have fallen deeper and faster than he'd intended.

A nap that had left him dead to the entire world was the worst thing he could have done. Anything could have happened while he was out. An invasion of his room. An invasion of hers. Instead of beating her fist against his door, she could be dead.

His head sank lower. He was going to be sick.

"Sam." His name drifted through the door,

lower now but with a firmness that brooked no argument. "Open the door."

"Go to sleep."

"Not until you—"

"I said no!"

The door was thin enough to let her soft gasp leak through. Regret instantly replaced the fear that still had his heart driving against his ribs. He hadn't yelled, but it had probably sounded that way, the harshness of the words evident even if they were quiet. It was probably the same tone Amy had heard from the men her mother had paraded in front of her and her twin sister.

Sam doubled over, fighting nausea born out of his abrupt awakening coupled with the truth that he truly was a horrible person.

With a grim sigh, he pushed himself up and twisted the lock, then took a stance by the hallway door, staring at the fire evacuation route. He didn't want to look her in the eye when she came in.

A slight squeak and a soft rustle, then the clean fragrance of hotel shampoo and soap drifted into the room. In some unexpected way, the generic scent washed over him with a warmth he'd never felt before. The process had started when he'd kissed her, the smoothing of the last ruffled pieces of his soul into place. Her presence loosened the bands around his chest so he could fill his lungs for the first time in years.

This was all too weird.

Amy didn't make an effort to be near him, which was for the best with the memory of that kiss flooding his brain on top of everything else.

From the soft sounds behind him, she'd taken a seat on the chair in the corner of the room farthest from where he stood. "How often do you have nightmares?"

He froze. He swallowed so hard, Amy had to be able to hear it from the other side of the room. *Every night.*

He wouldn't be telling her the truth though.

"Come on, Sam. We may have only known each other for a few months, but you have to admit they've been some pretty intense months. You watched me fall apart by the side of the road in the most humiliating way possible. You talked me out of a second and a third panic attack because you knew exactly what to do. You told me your story about…" Another soft gasp, this one sharper. "Wait. Was your story even true? About Lindsay?

Or were you lying in order to distract me so we could keep moving?"

There it was. Amy had handed him a way out. He could tell her he'd made everything up to help her focus. He could tell her the nightmare was brought on by the pain of a bullet grazing his leg, even though it hadn't broken skin and only throbbed a little bit. He could shut the door on every way he'd let her in, even pretending their kiss never happened. This twisted, emotional roller coaster ride could end here.

He'd read every possible exit route on the map—primary and alternate—before the answer slipped out. "Everything I told you is true."

"And the nightmares?"

"More often than I'd like." *Dude. Seriously?* Did his mouth no longer listen to the shut-up signals from his brain? This woman wasn't his friend or his therapist or... Actually, he'd never talked to his friends about Lindsay or any other part of his past and he'd never had a therapist, so maybe that was the reason Amy was able to dig into his psyche and root out all of his secrets. She was no threat to him... as long as he didn't kiss her again.

Or so he kept telling himself. It was starting to feel as though she'd hooked a finger around his heart and it would be painful to slip away. "Do you always barge into people's lives this way?"

"Only if I think I can help."

It fit with everything he knew about her, from the way she'd laid her life on the line in order to stop Grant Meyer from hurting anyone else, to the way she'd risked her neck once before and was willing to do so again in order to protect Layla. Amy Brady had a heart too big for her own good.

If she wasn't careful, her compassion would get her killed.

When Sam finally turned, she was sitting in the chair in the corner with her chin resting on her knees, which she'd pulled to her chest. Her blond hair hung loose and damp to her shoulders, framing a face scrubbed free of makeup so that a handful of freckles scattered across her nose. Her eyes...

Her eyes. Free of the eyeliner or mascara or whatever she'd worn around them earlier, her green eyes seemed to grow larger, the focal point of her very being. He could drown in those eyes if he wanted to. Could leap in and never come up for air.

It wouldn't be a bad way to go.

She shifted and looked away, toward the curtained balcony doors, and Sam jerked his head to the side. He'd been staring. After the way he'd turned his back on her after he'd kissed her, he had no right.

Sam cleared his throat. He was too tired for this. That was the problem. Between the months of watching to make sure she hadn't blown her identity and the intensity of the day, his head was toast. His emotions were out of whack. If he thought the woman in front of him was anything other than a mission, then it was definitely time to hit the rack and aim for some rest. "You should go next door and get some sleep. I left you some snacks and we'll try to get a real breakfast in the morning."

"I saw. Thank you." She didn't move to obey his order. Instead, she picked at a loose string on the hem of her pants and tucked her knees closer to her chest. "What happens next?"

Sam couldn't fault her for the question. He wasn't even sure he knew, but he needed to project control to her. Puffing his cheeks, he exhaled, then walked across the room and sat on the end of the bed closest to her, abasing his better judgment. "Ideally, we'd simply head to Washington and have you reassigned, train you with a new name, a new backstory and—"

"I really can't go back to Georgia?" The words were heavy, the tone resigned. "Ever?"

"You want to risk it?"

"I don't know. Honestly, I don't know anything right now." She dropped her forehead to her knees, the words muffled into her legs. "You said *ideally.* We're nowhere near an ideal situation, are we?"

"No."

"At least you're honest."

That was probably the only good thing he was. "I'm cut off from my team and anyone else in WITSEC until further notice. There's no sense in risking a hacked email or a traced phone call. It's kind of me and you against the world at the moment." He stood, stretched his arms over his head, then laid a hand on the back of her head and let a couple of silky strands of her hair filter through his fingers before he caught himself and backed away. "Right now, we're safe. If the threat to you is coming from the inside, then nobody can track us while we're outside of the box. If it's coming from the outside, they'll have to rely on dumb luck to locate us. Get some sleep and let me worry about what comes next, okay?"

It was a long moment before Amy moved, unwrapping her arms and straightening her legs. She was so tiny, even when she wasn't curled into a ball. Sam's gut instinct screamed to wrap his arms around her and shield her from whatever came in their direction next, but that was definitely light years past his job description. Instead, he walked to the door between their rooms and shoved her door fully open. She probably didn't want to face a dark night alone any more than he did, but there was no other choice. "Go ahead. In the morning, we can—"

An ear-jolting buzz blared into the room. Light flashed from the small red box on the wall. Instinctively, Sam jumped toward Amy as she slapped her hands over her ears.

The fire alarm. Either the building was burning, or someone had found them and was trying to smoke them out into the open, to make them targets with no place to hide.

ELEVEN

Amy's chest ached from her gasp at the horrible sound that had driven her hands to her ears. The pulsing buzz still found its way between her fingers and lodged in the center of her brain. Tears leaked from her eyes at the pain. Whoever had invented fire alarms had definitely known how to get attention. It figured one would go off tonight.

At least it wasn't her initial fear that a bomb had gone off. Nothing had exploded through the doorway.

Yet.

By the time she'd adjusted to the sound and cleared her vision, Sam stood between her and the door, his focus on the door. His pistol was at the ready, and his mouth was a grim line.

The truth sank in and Amy lowered her hands, watching the man who'd been tasked to protect her as he morphed into a fierce defender. She could read his thoughts all over his face as her mind reeled. He didn't believe the alarm was merely an alarm. "Sam?"

With his free hand, Sam aimed a finger at the corner near the bathroom and out of sight of the hall door. "Get over there. Stay low. Don't move once you're in position."

Amy rushed across the room on shaking legs, her hip catching the side of the dresser. Pain shot down her leg. She pressed her back into the corner, wedged between the wall and the nightstand as she watched Sam. There was only one reason for her to be tucked away like this. He wanted her out of the line of fire if someone started shooting through the door. Of course, that didn't leave him any protection, not where he was standing. He should be beside her, away from danger.

But keeping himself safe wasn't his job. His job was to stand between her and any threat.

How much longer could she let him do this? If he died because someone had come after her, Amy would never be able to live with herself. She should give up, walk out the door and turn herself over to whoever was doing this. It was her they were looking for, not Sam. No one else should be hurt because of her. She shifted, but a sharp look from Sam pressed her back against the wall once again. Based on the guilt he already carried, he'd hate himself forever if something happened to her on his watch. This was his calling, his mission. Failure would destroy him.

She was trapped…and so was he.

From the hallway came the sound of voices, barely audible above the blaring alarm. People were likely heading outside away from any smoke or flame. Shouldn't they be moving out too? If the building truly was on fire, they could die in a scene born out of her worst fears. Could she smell smoke, or was her imagination running on overtime?

She opened her mouth to ask, but Sam holstered his pistol and turned from the door. "I don't like this." He paced to the sliding doors that led to a small balcony. Edging to the side, he pulled the edge of the curtain away from the wall and peeked out, then let the heavy fabric drop into place. "This is too coincidental."

"You think someone found us?" *Probably.* This was the way her life worked now. She'd be on the run forever, hiding in remote hotels or even in the wilderness, trying to save a life that had ceased to be any sort of life at all.

Whose life was she trying to save anyway? Amy Brady was dead, the victim of a horrible car accident. Amy Naylor was no more. She didn't exist outside of this room. The truth made her wonder what exactly it was she was fighting to save.

"There's no way to know for sure, but I'm going to go with the worst-case scenario and assume someone has figured out we're here. At this point, we're better safe than sorry." He muttered something under his breath, then looked from the hall door to the balcony door. "If the goal is to get you out into the open, then I doubt they've actually set the place on fire. All that would do is make it harder for them to get inside and would make it harder for them to find you. It's more likely someone pulled a fire alarm and is waiting in the hallway or near a fire exit for us to make an appearance. The trick to getting out is choosing the entrance they're not watching. I have no way of knowing if anybody's really out there, where they are or how many they've got waiting." His words were more for himself than for her. It seemed to be a thing with him, talking through tense situations out loud. It likely was a way to help him think.

Sam drummed his fingers on his pistol at his hip, then strolled to the hall door, out of sight.

Amy slipped to the corner and peered around. He was studying the fire exit plan again, tracing lines with his finger. When he turned, he glanced from her to the balcony door, then back to the emergency routes. He tapped the plastic over the map. "The exits are here," he pointed to one end of the building, "And here." A finger tap on the other end and another at the front punctuated his declaration. "There's no exit out the back because of the pool and the air-conditioning units for the common areas."

"Okay..."

"If there's no exit out the back, then I doubt they'll look for us in the back. If we can get out that way somehow and slip to the truck while anyone watching would expect us to use the main exits at the front and sides, then we can get you clear." He strode to the balcony door and stared at the curtain.

Amy stood tall and crossed her arms over her stomach, trying to hold herself together. Her eyebrows raised so high they pulled her eyes even wider. She could almost see what he was thinking as a plan spun through his mind. "Are you about to suggest we...? No. I'm not going over a balcony railing and dangling into space like I'm in some kind of action movie. Come up with something else."

"You act like I've never done this before."

"I act like *what*?" She dropped her arms to her sides and stepped closer to him, eyeing the back of his head. If she stared hard enough, maybe she could see straight through to his thoughts. Hopefully, they'd be anything other than what she feared. "You've climbed over a balcony before?"

"More than once. It's not very hard, especially when you're in our situation and you're only going from the second floor to the first. Guys doing parkour do it all the time."

"They also climb the sides of buildings and jump between them for giggles. None of those things seem fun to me."

"It's not as hard as you'd think. The trick is in using your upper body strength, which your former personal trainer self should have plenty of. Before this night is over, you're going to figure out you have a set of skills you've never even tapped into. Maybe you'll discover a new hobby." He looked over his shoulder at her, his amusement fading quickly. "There may not be another way out. For all I know, someone is prowling the halls looking for you while we stand here and debate this thing. We could hunker down in here but I'm not certain that's the safest option when I have zero intel about the situation or even if there's a real fire." As if to punctuate his statement, sirens wailed in the distance. Lots of sirens. "This won't be the first time I've taken an asset over the side of a building, and it's a lot closer to the ground tonight than it ever has been before. I did some recon when we first got into our rooms. You'll be fine."

A chill wracked her, fear worming its way into her bones. "Sam…"

He ignored her, reaching for the black backpack on his bed and sliding it over his shoulders. "Slip over the railing, get your hands down as low as you can. There's a pole that runs along the corner of the balcony as a support. Slide down it until your feet hit the bottom rail. Think of it like you're in the playground as a kid on the climbing wall or something. You'll drop next to the fence that houses the AC units for the main areas downstairs. We'll crouch behind the fence, get a feel for the situation and get to the truck before anybody figures out we're gone or how we did it."

Had she mentioned to him she had a fear of heights on top of everything else? That she'd always hated sliding down that fireman's pole thing in elementary school?

Down the hall, a door slammed. Someone pounded on another door at the far end of the hall. "Fire department! Evacuate!"

Finger to his lips, Sam killed the lights in the room, grabbed Amy by the wrist and pulled her toward the balcony. "Fire department hasn't had time to get here yet," he whispered. "We have to move."

Okay, so even worse than her fear of heights was her fear of being murdered. She let him drag her to the balcony.

"Don't look down and you'll be fine." Sam slid the door open enough for them to slip through and led the way out, crouching low with his pistol drawn as he scanned the area. No one seemed to be in the parking lot at the rear of the building. Flashing lights and sirens appeared on the road to the left, racing closer. Smoke hung low, hazing the air.

Someone really had set a fire in the building.

Squeezing her hand, Sam turned toward

Amy, his eyes only inches from hers. "I'll go first. You stay low. If anything goes wrong, I'll catch you. I promise. Just watch what I do and imitate me." He started to move, then dropped back onto his heels again. "If anything happens to me, lock the door and forget about being anonymous any longer. Call the police." He squeezed her wrist, holstered his weapon and slipped over the railing. In mere seconds, his low hiss drifted up from the ground. "Now."

Amy took two deep breaths before she stood, slipped over the railing and held on tight, her back tensed against an imagined gunshot. Keeping her eyes in front of her, she gripped the thin bars and crouched low, then wrapped one arm around the thick metal pole. She stretched her foot down as far as she could, her toe brushing the rail of the bottom floor patio, then closed her eyes and let gravity inch her lower.

Strong hands gripped her waist and helped her the rest of the way, dragging her to the ground where she crouched with her back against Sam's chest, desperate to catch her breath. He leaned forward, his whisper warm on her ear and nearly drowned out by the air-conditioning unit on the other side of the fence. "You're not wearing shoes?"

The strength of his chest against her back warmed her from the inside out. Taking in air was impossible because he stole it as fast as she breathed it. This was not the time. Amy fought for her voice. "Really? That's your takeaway when I just almost plummeted to my death?"

"Drama queen." He tugged her to the side and crept toward the corner of the fence. "The truck's on the other—"

A gunshot cracked over the sound of the sirens and dirt shot up from the spot where Amy had been crouching seconds before. She screamed.

Sam ripped his gun from its holster and shoved her around the corner as another bullet splintered the wood fence inches from Amy's head.

Sam pulled Amy close to the side of the brick hotel building and rushed her toward Isaiah's truck parked at the far end of the lot. The shooter was above them on one of the balconies, but if Sam could keep Amy close to the building, the angle of fire would prevent their assailant from getting a clear shot.

To have found them so quickly, their anonymous attacker had to have known approximately which room they were in all along. Sam would love to step into the open and look up, to get a full view of whoever was attempting to murder Amy. He ached to do so, but he couldn't without slowing their forward momentum. Priority number one was getting Amy to safety. Discovering the identity of whoever was aiming a gun at them would have to wait until she was secure.

No more bullets cracked into the night, though shouts from the other side of the building indicated the evacuees in the far parking lot had heard.

Great. All Sam needed was some John Wayne trying to be a hero and landing himself in the line of fire. He urged Amy forward. "Keep moving." There was no way to know if the shooter had backup. They had to get out of the area before their enemy could mobilize and hem them in.

He also couldn't risk being stopped by a mob of frightened hotel guests who had likely already called 911 with reports of shots fired. He couldn't take the time to explain things to the police. If the hack to the WITSEC system ran as deep as Dana thought it did and they were held up fighting red tape at a police station, it would give whoever was trailing them time to mount an offensive.

Sam helped Amy into the truck and rounded to the driver's side, weapon at the ready even though no more shots came. Whoever had pulled the trigger might be acting alone and was headed down to try to prevent their escaping. Throwing his go-bag into the back seat, he jumped into the truck and jammed the key into the ignition. Sam jerked the vehicle into Reverse and skidded out of the space, pausing only to slam the gearshift into Drive.

The rear window shattered as the truck gained traction.

Amy screamed.

For the second time in too few hours, Sam shoved her head toward her knees. He gripped the steering wheel and tore around the side of the building in a skid he could barely hold. He had to get Amy to safety.

Amy clasped her hands at the back of her neck with her head nearly to the floor. "Is this really happening again?"

"I was thinking the same thing." At least she was vocal and not lost inside fear. If she was anything like him, she'd passed emotions and landed in a place void of feeling. It happened when the panic became too much. For him, his brain sought protection by distancing itself from reality and shutting down emotion. In some ways, the void was worse than the fear, but now Amy's detachment worked to their advantage. There wasn't time to calm her if she panicked.

Glancing in the rearview, Sam aimed Isaiah's truck toward the on-ramp and floored it. They were onto the highway, then off at the next exit, headed north into nowhere before he spoke again. "You can sit up. Nobody followed us."

Amy rose and swiped blond hair away from her forehead. She braced her hands on the dash and stared out the front window, almost as though she were trying to ground herself to something that wouldn't let her down. "How did they find us?"

It was the question he'd hoped she wouldn't ask. His theory was one he didn't like, and he wasn't exactly sure how to handle the situation if he was right.

"Sam? Don't clam up on me now. We've gone through too much together."

"We ditched everything you were carrying back at the college. I left my phone and radio behind. We have nothing we started out with."

"There's nothing left to track us with unless…" She jerked her hands from the dash as though it had burned her.

She was thinking the same thing he was. Somehow, someone had managed to track Isaiah's vehicle. "This is Isaiah's personal truck." It was also new, and Isaiah wasn't going to like the new ventilation in the rear. "It wouldn't be hard for a savvy hacker to find us via GPS." Although that didn't make sense. If they wanted Amy so badly, why set off the fire alarm? Why not simply wait for them to get back to the truck and take them out then? Or plant a bomb in the vehicle?

It felt as though someone was toying with them the way a cat would a mouse. Catch and release. Attack and withdraw. No, whoever it was couldn't be tracking the vehicle. It had to be something else, something he was missing.

"What do we do now?" Amy hunched in the seat, her head below the headrest, probably half to dodge the frigid air filling the cab through the broken window and half to keep herself hidden if more shots were fired.

"We should ditch the truck as soon as possible, even though I doubt it's the source. It's still the last known link someone can use to trace us." After that, he was still working out the plan. No matter the situation, there was always a way out. All he had to do was work through the scenarios and get them to safety. He would then be free to make contact with his team and get orders.

Sam desperately needed his team. He'd grown used to having people behind him, people who could trace calls and license plates, who could work three steps ahead of him to clear the way. This James Bond/Lone Ranger routine was a test of his abilities, a stretch of his skills. In one way, he welcomed the challenge. In another, he was desperate for backup. History had proven he didn't work well on his own.

He was no good alone. In the army, it had been all about the team, each member a piece in a moving machine. Those men had never failed to have his back. Barnes, Caesar, Rich…

Rich.

One hand gripping the wheel, Sam grabbed his go-bag and tossed it into Amy's lap. "There's a burner phone in there in the inside pocket. Turn it on and call the number I give you. Ask for Richardson. Tell him what's going on." He rattled off a number, then his voice dropped to a low mutter. "We're about to need all the help we can get."

Since they were winding up the side of a mountain, it was possible Amy wouldn't be able to get a signal to even make the call. Driving aimlessly wasn't his favorite way to spend a night, and he needed another set of eyes. At the rate they were going, without outside help, they'd be dead before morning.

"This must be someone you trust a lot if—" She broke off and her tone shifted. "Is this Richardson?"

"Tell him you're with me and you need a vehicle and a place to lay low."

She relayed the information, slouching deeper into the seat as she shivered against the cold. "He wants to know if you need him to come to you or if you can come to him."

There was the solution to the vehicle problem. Ditch the truck and hitch a ride with Rich, an old army buddy who'd been through the darkest times with him. "Tell him to come to us." If they could meet him without being followed, this would work. Without the truck, they'd be off the radar and completely untraceable.

"He wants to know how much gas you have."

Sam glanced at the gauge. "Between half and three-quarters." Thankfully, it had been full when Isaiah tossed him the keys.

As she relayed the information, Sam fought curves, wary of bleeding off speed. He was itching to talk to Rich himself, but this phone wasn't connected to Bluetooth and he didn't dare take a hand from the wheel. Besides, he didn't want Amy to hear anything he had to say, any conjectures he had to make. She'd panicked already, and though she seemed to be holding it together now, they didn't have time to make a roadside stop.

Through the phone, the hum of Rich's voice talked, paused, then went on some more, loud enough to hear his voice but not loud enough to decipher the words. Sam massaged the steering wheel and dug his teeth into his tongue to keep from moving the conversation along. Lindsay had always accused him of having control issues and Sam had never denied it, especially not in situations like this. He needed instruction, direction, something solid before headlights could show up behind them.

Although they may not have a tail at all. If whoever was shooting at them was somehow tracking the vehicle, it was only reasonable to think they wouldn't give chase. They'd simply wait to strike again at the next stop. "Tell him to give me a meeting location but not to make it obvious. Code it. I'm not sure yet if the bad guys are listening in." The truck could merely be bugged.

But how?

Amy relayed the message, then listened for a moment. "He said to tell you 'blue and gold, fifty-seven, 0430.'"

"Blue and gold, fifty-seven, 0430." Sam scanned the road in front of him, trying to see the words, to make pictures out of them. The silence hung thick, both in the truck and over the phone as Rich waited. He was trying to direct them to safety but…

0430 made sense. Military time. Four thirty in the morning. But *blue and gold, fifty-seven*? Fifty-seven… The number tickled. He tried to put the colors and numbers together into one picture. Caught a flash of memory, the number fifty-seven in gold on a royal blue field of color.

He almost snapped his fingers. Riley Eldridge, Rich's cousin. Deep in the North Carolina mountains, about forty minutes outside of Asheville, there was a dirt racetrack near Asher Creek where they'd once gone to see

Riley race. She drove a blue-and-gold dirt track race car. Number fifty-seven.

"Got it. Tell him I'm going dark."

Amy relayed the affirmation, then ended the call. She started to settle the phone into the cup holder, but Sam held out his hand. When the weight of the device was settled on his palm, he rolled down the window and chucked it into the night. He couldn't risk a trace, even on a burner.

Amy gasped, then she actually chuckled. "Drastic times."

Yeah, she'd sunk into that place past exhaustion if she was laughing when there was absolutely nothing to amuse her. Sam glanced her way.

She drew her arms tighter around herself as the truck's heater fought valiantly against the cold air seeping in through the back window. It was losing the battle.

"There's probably a sweatshirt in my backpack if you want to grab it."

As Amy reached behind her, Sam hung a left on a road that should lead them toward Asher Creek, the invisible bands around his chest loosening a bit.

He didn't relax too much. If someone truly was tracking them, tossing his phone wasn't enough. There was no good way to hide until they'd abandoned this vehicle. If they were confronted on the road, the results would be deadly. This deep in the back mountains in weather this frigid, there were two options available to their would-be killer. He'd either engage them in a blind shootout or run them off the side of a cliff. Neither was an option Sam wanted to explore.

Because no matter how he played either of those scenarios in his head, both outcomes ended with Amy dead.

TWELVE

"Amy."

Her name drifted in from far away, somewhere in the deep recesses of a dream that refused to shake loose.

No, not a dream. A nightmare. Someone was chasing her. Shooting at her. Dragging her over a steep cliff into darkness...

She sat up suddenly, her forehead colliding with something hard. Something that muttered a deep, growling, "Watch it."

Her eyes popped open and stared into brown ones only inches away. Brown eyes narrowed with pain.

Sam. He sat back and rubbed his chin where her forehead must have connected.

Last night rushed back. The fire alarm at the hotel, the climb over the balcony railing, the back windshield shattering, his kiss...

Instinctively, she touched his shoulder,

but he backed away so quickly he nearly lost his balance. Her hand fell to the bed. No, it wasn't a bed. This was a cot, but figuring out how she'd gotten here could wait. "Where are we?"

One side of his mouth tipped up in a smile. "You fell asleep in the truck."

"I fell asleep?"

"Deep sleep. I had to carry you. You didn't move when we switched trucks or when I brought you inside." He turned and walked across the room to the door. "Rich and I thought you'd never wake up. And by the way—" he paused with his hand on the door frame "—you snore." He disappeared before she could get her bearings enough to respond.

She snored? Was he making a joke? It was hard to tell with the way he spoke, his voice monotone, his back to her. In some ways, he seemed to get a kick out of this whole mess they were in. In others, this had to be a giant pain for him. After all, he'd had to haul her into this cabin after...

Wait. He'd carried her?

Her brain was too sleep-drugged to deal with the thought of Sam lifting her in his arms, especially when his kiss had been one of the first things she'd thought of when she'd seen him. Her mind was inclined to believe things it shouldn't about a man who'd saved her life at the peril of his own.

Amy needed to remember her mother's mistakes, to be sure she didn't repeat them.

She stared at the door Sam had exited through, then shook the thoughts away, dragging her palms down her face in a fight to get her bearings. The dark cold interior of the pickup hung over her existence as her last clear memory. His sweatshirt, warm from both the soft fabric and the slight spicy scent of Sam's cologne. She ran her hands down the arms of the shirt as her senses struggled to catch up to her surroundings. Her brain was reluctant to believe she wasn't still in a truck careening down a mountain while she dreamed of this place.

If she were dreaming, hopefully her brain would choose better than this. Rough wooden walls enclosed a room that held a low dresser and the metal-framed cot where she'd slept in her clothes, covered by a green wool blanket stamped with a faded *US ARMY*. The room wasn't exactly warm, but the chill had less of an edge than the truck had held.

Sam had carried her into this place and she'd been so dead to the world that she hadn't even known. Amy scrubbed at her face again, desperate to wipe away the hot embarrassment in her cheeks. She never slept that hard, ever. At least not in the past three years, and especially not after someone took a shot at her. It felt as though she'd lived her life with one eye open, always expecting the worst. With last night being the embodiment of *the worst*, how had her brain let its guard down? Anything could have happened while she was zonked in dreamland.

Somehow her subconscious truly trusted Sam and his friend Rich, at least enough to let her sleep. None of this made any sense.

Neither did the tantalizing aroma wafting through the door. Was that bacon? They were running for their lives with nothing to their names and, at least in her case, no shoes on their feet. How had Sam managed to find bacon?

It didn't matter. Her stomach demanded she get off the increasingly uncomfortable cot and locate whatever was cooking somewhere in this rustic cabin...even if it meant facing Sam and the memory of that kiss.

Shoving her hands through her hair in a vain effort to shake out the tangles, Amy made her way into a large open living area that housed a tiny kitchen, a four-person table and two garish floral-print sofas that had seen their better days in the '70s. A thin pillow and another wool blanket covered one of the couches, probably where Sam had slept. Three more doors stood closed around the small cabin space, and the rough hardwood floors creaked beneath her feet.

Sam turned from the small stove and set a plate of eggs on the table next to a thick orange mug of heavy black coffee. "Bacon will be up in a second."

Sliding into a chair, Amy rested her chin on her fist. This had to be a dream. Or a nightmare. It no longer mattered. Apparently, she and Sam were in this together, and he hadn't answered her earlier question. Well, he didn't get to dodge her. It was her life in danger, not his. "I'm asking again. Where are we?"

"Rich had a pretty genius idea." He kept his back to her, fussing with a sizzling pan on the stove.

Fine then. He'd answer when he was ready. She'd had enough psychology classes to puzzle this one out. Deputy Marshal Sam Maldonado liked control. Refusing to answer her was either a professional habit or an incredibly annoying side effect of his need to be in charge.

She watched him work at the stove, letting her mind drift, too tired to direct her thoughts. Whatever Sam had done in the army before he moved over to the Marshals Service, the work had been good to him. His back and shoulders were strong beneath a gray T-shirt. His brown hair was sleep-rumpled, giving him the appearance of a college kid who was past caring about appearances during a stressful exam week. When he finally turned, his brown eyes struck her again, catching her attention the way they had the first time she'd ever seen him.

They seemed to see right through her.

He walked to the table and slid into the chair across from Amy's, dropping a plate of bacon between them onto the scarred blond wood. "Eat. You're bound to be hungry, and I don't know how long we'll be here. The timing of our next meal could be iffy."

"You're all personality before you get your coffee, aren't you?" She wasn't a morning person either, but honestly, he could be a little bit friendlier.

"Nice can get you killed."

Alrighty then. Gone was the Sam who had

shared his thoughts with her the night before, the Sam who had looked at her as though there were things he wasn't saying.

The Sam who had kissed her. She was now hiding out with a hard-boiled film noir detective. The joy.

Amy reached for her coffee and took a cautious sip. It was hot and strong. Not the way she liked it, but there was no way the man had scrounged up cream along with bacon and eggs. "Where is your friend Rich?" He had to be around somewhere. If he was anything like Sam, it was highly doubtful he'd dumped them off and run.

"He's keeping an eye on things outside. He's more familiar with this area than I am."

"And where is *this area*?"

"We're several miles outside of a little town called Asher Creek, halfway up a mountain in some pretty thick woods. Rich's cousin Riley lives nearby. This is her fiancé, Zach's, place. He's prior service military as well. He came by earlier and dropped off some food and a bag of clothes that belong to Riley, even some shoes. I figure y'all are close enough to the same size." Sam took a sip of coffee. "We're safe for the moment, but since I have no idea how they tracked us before, I can't say for how long."

Amy set her coffee mug next to the thick white plate of rapidly cooling eggs, the sight and scent overwhelming her stomach. "Any more clues on how they keep finding us?"

"We're safe unless one of us has some random implant we don't know about." He seemed to almost smile, then simply shrugged. "I left the truck at a racetrack on the south side of Asher Creek, about forty-five minutes from here. Hopefully, they'll assume we continued to head north toward DC."

The whole situation made little sense. She knew how this worked. There should be other marshals. Backup. Redundancies. "Why are we stuck out here alone?"

"Because we don't know how deeply we've been compromised or if someone inside is involved." Sam slid a piece of bacon from one side of his plate to the other. "The issue is deep enough for us to be found and to compromise a safe house. Keeping you off the grid is our safest course of action right now. You're not the only one. Around the country, we've got other witnesses being shuffled and double-guarded as we speak." He shoved in a bite of eggs, then aimed his fork at her plate. "Seriously. You need to eat."

He was so casual about it all. *WITSEC could be compromised. We're totally cut off from help. I'm cooking breakfast in a cabin for the girl who nearly got me killed. How's the weather?*

Picking up her fork, Amy shoved the eggs around her plate, then reached for a slice of bacon instead. Maybe it would sit better in her stomach.

Sam wiped his hands on a paper towel, then dropped it to the table. "I know you've told me a bit about this other witness, Layla, but if you're willing to talk it might give us some new information I can pass on to my team when we're able to make contact again. If you'll let me, we can bring her in to safety."

"At this point, you and your team probably already know more than I do."

"How about we try anyway? You can start at the beginning." He tipped his chin at her plate. "While you eat."

He might be right, but he sure was bossy. Amy loudly crunched a piece of bacon. It was crispy, practically shattering in her mouth, exactly the way she liked it. *There, I ate a bite. Happy?* "First, tell me why I should trust these people I've never met. You've mentioned Rich, Riley, Zach…"

"If you can trust me, you can trust them. I do. What's to question?" The words were cocky, but uncertainty clouded his expression. He reached for his coffee and drained the cup, then got up from the table and went the counter. He refilled his mug but kept his back to her, facing the window as he spoke. "I don't know how much weight this carries with you given it's been three years since you last saw her, but Rich knows your sister."

"Eve?" Amy's heart crashed against her rib cage, fueled by grief and longing, along with the familiar fear the bitterness her twin sister might harbor. "Rich knows Eve?"

"Remember, she goes by Jenna." Sam set his coffee on the table and looked at something over her shoulder. "We should talk about her. You need to know everything that's happened."

"Everything? There's more than what you told me last night?"

Shoving his coffee cup to the side, Sam reached for her hand, then drew back, clasped his hands on the table. "Grant Meyer was arrested because of your sister. Several months ago, he went on an all-out blitz to eliminate you. He had the wrong woman. Amy, Grant Meyer went to jail because he kidnapped and tried to murder your sister."

"No." Amy's voice, thin and weak, barely reached Sam's ears. She shoved the chair away with the screech of wood against wood and paced into the middle of the small living area, her arms wrapped tightly around herself, his sweatshirt dwarfing her.

Did she realize she was still wearing it? Last night, he'd suggested she grab it because the truck's heat couldn't keep up with the brutal cold flooding in through the shattered window.

This morning, seeing her in his navy blue hoodie with *Colorado* emblazoned across it in bold white letters felt as though they were somehow more than endangered witness and assigned marshal.

Kissing her hadn't helped.

Before Sam met her, when she'd first disappeared months ago, Sam had studied her file and talked to her twin sister, learning everything he could. He'd spent time with her during meetings with Edgecombe. He'd watched her sleep in his truck, fully aware of the trust her rest implied. She might talk a big game and be fond of questioning him, but she trusted him.

She'd given him a gift, a piece of her heart he was supposed to protect along with the rest of her, from a threat that was still very real.

There was the problem. The threat to her life was still in motion. This was still a situation where the forty-two second countdown could start at any moment. He shouldn't be having thoughts about her outside of his job. He'd retrieved and protected dozens of witnesses and fugitives in his five years on the US Marshals Service's elite recovery team. Never once had he become personally involved.

He'd definitely never kissed a witness. Had never even desired to.

But as Amy Brady paced the living room and stopped to stare into the stone-cold fireplace, Sam wanted nothing more than to walk across the room and hug her. To make her feel better. To restore color to her cheeks, which had grown incredibly pale when he'd dropped the bombshell about her twin. On top of multiple brushes with her own mortality the night before, this news had to be devastating.

Sam was halfway to her before he stopped himself in an awkward spot between the kitchen table and the couch. He shouldn't. It didn't matter that something about her drew him closer. She wasn't his friend. She wasn't the woman he loved. She was his assignment and nothing more. Once they figured out who was tracking them, he'd turn Amy over to the main team assigned to her case and walk away, never to see her again. That was the way this job worked.

Besides, she didn't need to get close to a guy like him, one whose tortured thoughts dogged him all day and kept him awake all night. One who couldn't sleep without the nightmares of his failures, without the blood on his hands returning to haunt him over and over again.

In all honesty, she deserved a better protector than him as well. His game was off. Lack of sleep and fear had dulled his carefully honed edge.

Sam stalked to the kitchen table, picked up his coffee mug and drained it. The liquid burned all the way down, searing the truth into his core.

Fear. Fear was the reason Amy Brady was different than any other person he'd been tasked to protect. Last night by the side of the road, her fear had reached out and gripped the same emotion that laid inside of him, waiting to pounce. He'd laid his hands on her shoulders, looked her in the eye and seen himself. In that moment, he'd lost a piece of his heart to her.

Now, she stood less than twenty feet away with her hands drawn into the sleeves of his sweatshirt, probably because they were shaking and cold.

He knew the feeling, knew the way fear could burst from inside with the force and heat of a volcano or could creep up from the core, icy and paralyzing.

No way could he leave her alone to process the turns of her life. He might be a failure, but he wasn't a monster.

Sam slammed the mug to the table and stalked across the room before he could change his mind. He pulled Amy close, her head tucked beneath his chin and her hands balled into fists against his chest. His fingers splayed across the middle of her back.

She was shaking. For several heartbeats, Sam simply held her, then he shifted and rested his chin on the top of her head. She was so tiny and, despite all of her fight, so fragile.

He would protect her from Grant Meyer's

people if he had to die doing so. The ferocity of the truth almost knocked him backward, but he held on, unwilling to let Amy feel him crack.

"Is she okay?" Amy's voice muffled against his shoulder, more feeling than sound.

"She's safe." The truth could wait. She was safe, but she was likely under police protection until federal agents figured out who was behind these attacks. Jenna wasn't Amy, but there was nothing to stop someone from using one twin to draw the other into the open.

Amy nodded. Although he'd expected her to pull away, she stayed close, her shivers subsiding as she rested in his arms. Sam let her rest, drawing comfort from her. There was something about her that reached inside of him and made him feel twice as tall and three times as strong as he was. He could almost forget his past mistakes, could almost hope there was a way to start again.

With her.

"She was in danger because of me, because Meyer thought she was me."

"But now his organization knows she's not."

Amy laughed, a sharp bark that sounded as though it came from the darkest well of her fear. "Is that supposed to make me feel better? The killers know Grant got the wrong girl so now they're coming after the right one?" She shoved his chest and turned away, her shoulders a rigid line.

Sam didn't know what to do. Naturally, in trying to make it all better, he'd made everything worse.

But then her shoulders slumped and she breathed deeply, turning to him. Her gaze remained on his chest. "Okay, so the fact that Eve is safe now does help. Or *Jenna* is safe. That's what she's calling herself now?"

"Yes. Jenna Clark. You'll have to get used to that one. She's not going back to the old name."

"Why not?"

"She wanted to cut ties with who Eve Brady was and what she stood for." Maybe he shouldn't have said it, but Amy seemed to put a premium on honesty.

Amy sank to the couch, burying her hands between her knees. The way she looked up at him was so plaintive and weak. "This is all my fault."

"That's not true." Sam dragged the heavy wooden coffee table closer and sat in front of her, their knees nearly touching. "She left

El Paso because a man she thought loved her tried to kill her. And that—" he held up his hand with his palm toward her to stop the argument she was about to pitch his way "—that was not your fault. You had no idea who Logan Cutter really was or what he was capable of. You met a seemingly nice man and introduced him to your sister. According to her, you tried to warn her about what Logan Cutter was doing when you found out, but she was in so deep by then that she cut you off and wouldn't listen to anything you had to say. He had her brainwashed, believing he was all she needed. Amy, that is nowhere near your fault. It's the fault of a man who preyed on your sister and sought to destroy her."

Her chin lifted, and her eyebrow arched over those clear green eyes of hers. "How do you know all of those things? There's no way they were in the mysterious file about me that you keep mentioning."

"I talked to Jenna a number of times when I was searching for you. She was worried about you. She wanted to see you, but WITSEC rules—"

"No." Amy stood and brushed past him. At the kitchen table, she collected their dishes and scraped the food into the trash can, then went to the sink with the plates. "Never. Not even if I get my life back."

"Why not?"

"Because my choices caused her pain. They nearly got her killed more than once. She's better off without me in her life. You said so yourself. She's keeping her new name because she wants to cut ties with the old one. The best thing for us to do is to move on."

She was completely misunderstanding everything he was saying. It was probably deliberate, a defense mechanism. He'd done the same thing with Lindsay at one time. "Okay. You don't have to see her until you're ready."

"I said never." The ceramic plates she'd been holding clattered into the sink. Amy wrapped her fingers around the edge of the counter and stared out the window.

There was more to this than she was saying. This was bigger than her sister. She was in pain, spiritual or emotional; it radiated from inside her and tugged at Sam's heart. Forget professional. He cared about her, there was no denying it, and he couldn't stand to see her suffer. Sam slipped around the table and laid his hands on her shoulders. "What's really going on?"

"Stop it." Amy ducked away from him and

backed toward her room. "Stop being nice to me. Stop caring about me!"

"Why?" He shouldn't care this much, shouldn't hurt this much, but he did. All he wanted was to rescue Amy, not only from a faceless killer but from herself.

"Why?" She shook her head, stared at the ceiling, refused to meet his eyes. "Because I'm a murderer."

THIRTEEN

The entire world seemed to hold its breath in a moment frozen in time.

There, she'd said it. She'd said it out loud and Sam could hate her now. He could stop looking at her as though he wanted to kiss her again or to care about her or whatever that look was that was slowly killing her inside. She dared to peek at him.

Sam held her gaze. His brown eyes narrowed slightly, as though he were trying to read the true meaning of her words. His lips were drawn tight, but it was more like in patient waiting than shock or anger.

Amy couldn't tear her eyes from him. If she confessed to all of her sins, explained herself, said the words banging on the door, begging to be let out, he would never look at her the same again. The beginnings of interest he'd shown her before would die, murdered by her sins.

It was what she wanted…and what she feared most. Because Sam Maldonado had managed to reach into her heart and make her feel again. Had managed to make her dream that someday she could be someone again.

That someday she could love, not with the disastrous twisted thing her mother had called love, but with real devoted love.

And she didn't deserve it, not after what she'd done not only to her sister, but to so many other young women just like her.

With one last look of longing at Sam, she made her decision. Sam needed to know the truth, because he deserved so much better than her. Amy swallowed the last of her pride and her hope, the last of the dreams she'd never even realized she'd dreamed. She drew her shoulders back. She was ripping off this bandage no matter how much pain it caused her.

She wanted to yell, but when she tried, the words were forced out past a swollen lump in her throat, the pain driving them to a hoarse, frightening whisper. "You don't know what I've seen."

Sam stepped forward. "I—"

"Worse, you don't know what I've done." Amy held up a hand to block him. "You have no idea. None. It can't be forgiven. It can't be swept under the rug. The federal government—your people—protected me, called me a witness and a hero but I'm just as guilty as the rest of them."

Sam's head swung back and forth, denying the truth. A blind loyalty she didn't deserve.

"I ran the office at New Horizons. I signed off on every *shipment* that arrived. I handed out every paycheck to every employee, and most of them turned around and handed those checks right back to the company, because they weren't getting paid. They thought they were working toward paying off a debt, but Grant and Logan never intended to set them free." She flipped her hand out and called the words like she was PT Barnum himself. "I even worked the weekends, recruiting women and men to sign up for a free week at the greatest spa in the world. And they signed up. And they were photographed. Blackmailed. Some of them were…were…" The words wouldn't come. *Trafficked.* They were trafficked. Ripped into a twisted world where human beings were commodities.

Every muscle in her body, every thought

in her mind screamed for her to meet Sam's eye, to see his reaction to her confession, but she couldn't. His disgust would destroy her.

Instead, she jammed her thumb into her chest, emphasizing each of her next words with a distinct, sharp jab. "I'm as guilty as they are." Her hand dropped to her thigh with a slap, her gaze landing on the floor at her feet.

"You didn't know." Sam's words were low, filled with compassion. "You did the job you were paid to do. Nobody told you the truth. And when you found out…" A rustle. Footsteps. Sam's boots appeared in front of her, then his hands were on her shoulders. "And when you found out, you made it right. You did everything you could to make sure Grant Meyer and Logan Cutter never harmed another person ever. Because of you, dozens of people are free. Amy…" Something in Sam's touch forced Amy to lift her head and meet brown eyes that held only understanding and another emotion she didn't want to analyze. "You did nothing wrong."

"I did everything wrong." Amy threw her hands up and tried to break Sam's hold on her, but he didn't let go.

"I'm not going to let you keep believing

this. Not for another second." He pressed a kiss to her forehead, his touch bringing the sting of tears to her eyes. "You have to forgive yourself."

"God can't even forgive me for—"

"Stop it." He slipped his hands up her neck to her cheeks, gently cradling them in his palms and forcing her to look at him. "That's silly talk and you know it. You need to hash this out with Him, but I can promise you He'll forgive you. I promise. It's the whole reason grace exists."

She dropped her gaze to his neck. He didn't understand. She should have known sooner what was happening right in front of her at the day spa. Should have stopped Grant and Logan sooner. Should have seen what Layla was going through before the other woman had had to tell her.

"And the second part is, you have to forgive yourself. You can't keep beating yourself up over this. You did what was right as soon as you found out what was going on. How could you have known sooner what Meyer and Cutter were up to? And even if you did…" He lifted her chin to force her to meet his eye. "You're not responsible for the actions of other people."

No, he didn't understand. He never would. As much as Amy wanted to believe him, wanted to sink into what he was offering her, both from God and from himself, she couldn't. In the end, he'd see her for who she really was, how she continually hurt the ones she was supposed to care for, and he'd either get hurt or he'd grow disgusted and leave.

"Forgive myself?" She stepped back, the words she was formulating slicing her own heart before she could even say them. "Don't give me advice you aren't willing to follow yourself."

Without looking back, Amy walked into her room, shut the door behind her, slid to the floor and cried.

Sam banged his fist against the countertop, the sting of the impact racing up his arm into his shoulder. It almost felt good, a distraction from the deeper pain working its way through his body with every beat of his heart.

"You know, if you break your hand you really aren't going to be doing anybody any good."

Flexing his fingers, Sam rolled his eyes to the ceiling but didn't turn toward the voice at the front door of the cabin. Go figure, the way his day was going. He should have known Rich would have managed to wander into ear-shot in time to hear him crash and burn with Amy. "You heard everything?"

"I heard enough."

"Figures." Fabulous. Not only was he losing Amy, but one of his oldest friends had been witness to his failure to make her feel safe and protected.

"Is there any coffee left? You dragged me out at all hours last night and set me up on guard duty today. Even the army offered up caffeinated sludge to take care of the lack of sleep."

"There's some left. Mugs are above the coffee pot." He probably already knew that, but Sam needed something to say.

The floor creaked as Rich walked into the room and crossed into the kitchen. From the sound of it, he poured two mugs and thunked them both on the table. "You look like you could use some more yourself. Either that or you need to trust me enough to keep an eye on things while you hit the rack for a bit. I'm pretty sure you threw that pillow and blanket over there on the couch for show and didn't sleep a wink."

This was the danger of working with a

team. For the last years of Sam's army career, Rich had been the teammate he'd been
closest to. They'd developed a rhythm, able to
read one another's thoughts in their actions,
on and off the battlefield. With the murder of
Rich's fiancée the year prior, it seemed the
man had only grown more introspective and
intuitive. He was definitely quieter. He used
to be the life of the party, the first to crack a
joke or to suggest a last-minute weekend at
the beach or in the mountains. With Amber's
death, Rich had matured, even aged a little.

He was right. Sam needed sleep. But between the nightmares and the constant need
for vigilance in order to keep Amy alive,
he knew sleep wouldn't come or, if it did,
it would only make everything worse. "I'm
good, but I'll take the coffee." He pulled one
of the wooden chairs away from the table and
slouched into it, reaching for the mug with
one hand and letting it warm his palm.

In his peripheral vision, Rich sipped his
coffee. "What's your plan?"

Straight to the point. It was the question
Sam wished he could answer. "I'm supposed
to get Amy to DC as soon as I'm cleared. It's
the safest place. In fact, I should probably be
headed that way with her now."

"Except that's the direction they'd expect you to head."

"Precisely."

"And you can't call in air support and chopper her out because…"

"Because I've been ordered to stay dark." Sam outlined the hack in the system and the complications it presented. "If I reach out and I give our location and someone on the inside is involved, we're in trouble, even over a secure server. Because I promise you, the way things have been going, whoever is out there is probably closer than help is."

"And this hack is the same reason I can't call in for you."

Sam tapped his nose and pointed at Rich. "You're on it. We'll lay low here for forty-eight hours and if they don't reach out by then I'll have you reach out for me. I'm not quite ready to tip off that I've got another burner in my go-bag." He'd packed that one himself months ago as insurance, tucked into a side compartment, no one on the inside or the outside knew he had it.

"I'm here for you, brother. You just let me know what you need."

"Manpower, mostly. What you've been doing. Combing the woods, being my eyes on the outside. Between you during the day and Riley's fiancé, Zach, at night, we should be able to keep Amy out of the line of fire."

Rich swigged his coffee and stared into the cup, making a face. "She's right, you know."

"Who's right?"

"Amy. You really shouldn't be handing out advice you aren't willing to follow yourself."

"Hmm." There was the turn in the conversation he'd been expecting when Rich first settled in. For a minute, he'd thought Rich was going to let him off without bringing it up. Sam tapped his index finger against the mug. "Nothing like gossiping over good coffee, huh?"

Rich chuckled. "Get real, Maldonado. No one on the planet would drink the sludge you call coffee. Not unless they were desperate. You might be long done with the military, but you still make it like Fitz always did. The spoon stands straight up in the mug before it dissolves."

Amy had drunk part of her coffee, but she was also probably desperate so there was really no argument to be made there. In fact, there was really no argument to be made at all. From experience, Sam knew Rich. And Rich was going to say his piece whether or not Sam wanted to listen. So he waited, hot mug burning his palm, afraid if he let go he'd have nothing left to hide behind.

"So, you met Jenna, Amy's sister?" Rich asked.

Sam's eyebrows lowered. This wasn't the direction Sam had expected the conversation to go. He nodded. Whatever Rich was getting around to, he'd get there eventually.

"You met the guy she's engaged to? Wyatt Stevens?"

Once. The Mountain Springs police officer had been present the one time Sam had met face-to-face with Jenna. A prior service man himself, Wyatt Stevens had seemed like a squared-away cop who loved Jenna with the kind of fierce love Sam envied, the kind he wished he could feel for another person.

The kind he felt for Amy. His mind seized on the thought and refused to let go. His hand dropped to the table, and he pulled it back as though the coffee mug had suddenly caught fire.

He was in love with Amy Brady. Had been for as long as he'd known her, when he'd realized the depth of her bravery and her loyalty. It was the reason he'd asked to work with Edgecombe. In his mind and on paper, he'd convinced himself and Deputy Marshall Watkins that it was to make sure Amy didn't take off again, to protect her in the event her identity had been compromised by her flight out of Georgia. But in his heart...

In his heart, it was because he couldn't imagine never seeing her again. And the more time he'd spent with her, the more he was drawn to her. The more he knew he'd die to protect her, not because it was his job but because he couldn't fathom this life without her, because she was everything he'd always wanted and she made him believe he could be the man he'd always imagined himself to be.

Rich simply sat back in his chair and sipped his coffee, his gray eyes holding slight amusement, the kind he seemed to have been missing when Sam had met with him a few months ago after Grant Meyer had tried to murder Jenna Clark. After a long enough dramatic pause, Rich settled his coffee mug onto the table and made a show of squaring it in front of him. "You're in love with her."

"Say that a little bit louder next time, why don't you?" Sam looked over his shoulder to make sure the door to Amy's room remained closed. "And I can't be."

"There's no reason you can't." When Sam

started to argue his point, Rich held up a hand, then crossed his arms over his chest, settling in his chair as though this were a normal day and they were about to have a normal chat. "I asked if you'd met Wyatt. Here's why. Back when Meyer was coming after Jenna, I told Wyatt he needed to back off, not to let his feelings for Jenna get the better of him or else he wouldn't be able to protect her. Fact is, I was wrong. Dead wrong. If he'd listened to me, he'd be a miserable man right now because he'd have pushed away the woman God intended him to be with. It would have been my fault."

"Which has nothing to do with me." Sam shoved away from the table and poured the rest of his coffee down the drain. He was edgy enough already, his insides bouncing like they were receiving electric shocks. More caffeine wasn't going to help. He glanced at Amy's door, then lowered his voice as he stared into the sink. "Being in love with Amy is out of the question. She's going to move on to a whole other protected identity in WITSEC. I'll move on to another mission. We'll never see each other again once this is over."

"'O ye of little faith.' Trust the process. If

God intended you to be together, you will be, just like Jenna and Wyatt."

"What about you and Amber?" Sam turned and leaned against the counter, watching the back of Rich's head. He wasn't trying to be mean. It was a genuine question. "Why is it some dreams we want work out and some dreams…" *Die.*

Rich sniffed and turned around, hooking his elbow over the back of his chair. "Can't answer that. Can only say that I spent months blaming myself for what Fitz's wife did to Amber. I took the blame for her murder. I should have been there. I should have done more. I should have seen it coming. Fact is, there was nothing I could have done. It was Jenna that finally helped me see the truth. Take that little conversation you and Amy just had and mush it all together and you get a point both of you said with your mouths but neither of you is actually living in your lives. Forgiveness, Maldonado. You have to forgive yourself."

"I blew it. I wasn't enough for Lindsay. I didn't take any of her feelings into account. And I was too late to save Devin Wallace. Even his brother blamed me and rightly so." Rich had heard the story. In fact, he was the only one Sam had poured the truth about Devin's death out to, not long after it happened, needing to have someone hear him lay out his sins, possibly offer him some sort of atonement.

"So you were supposed to know ahead of time that this Wallace character was going to break the rules. Maldonado, that was all on him. He knew better than to reach out to old contacts. You guys briefed him over and over against it. He's the one who did wrong. You did what you could to save him. And as for Lindsay—" Rich shrugged as though he didn't know what to say "—you both messed that one up. But if I remember right, that was in your pre-Jesus days. I'm guessing if you and Lindsay were still married, you'd both handle everything differently."

Sam shoved his hands into his pockets and stared at Amy's tightly closed door. "Maybe." When Rich leveled him with one of those looks he'd used on the battlefield more than once to muster the troops, Sam gave up. "Okay, yes."

Draining his cup, Rich set it on the table and stood. He pulled his coat from the back of the chair and shrugged it on. "I'm going out to keep an eye on things. As for you, you have two choices."

"You know you only outranked me by a couple of months when we were in the army, so you really can't give me ultimatums here."

"I still outranked you." Rich zipped his jacket and checked his pistol at his hip. "You either hit the rack and get some sleep or you talk to Amy and you guys hash this out once and for all. Because if you keep tying yourself up in knots and wasting your mental energy on this, then you really are going to miss the thing that gets her killed."

FOURTEEN

You're in love with her.

The words, spoken in an unfamiliar male voice—probably Rich's—had drifted through the door where Amy still sat with her head buried between her knees. Whatever the conversation was before and after those words, she hadn't been able to make it out. But those five words had come through as clearly as if Rich had spoken them in her ear.

You're in love with her.

The conversation after his statement hadn't been audible, although she'd strained to hear it. She'd finally given up and folded in half again. They couldn't have been talking about her. Maybe Sam was still in love with his ex-wife. Or maybe he had feelings for Dana, who was graceful and intelligent in a way Amy envied.

But if either of those other women had

Sam's heart, he wouldn't have kissed her. He was a better man than that. After all that she and Sam had been through, after the way he'd looked at her just now in the small kitchen, as though he'd wanted to repeat the kiss from the night before...

And she'd have let him repeat it. Gladly. More than once. For the rest of her life even.

As much as she wanted to sink into that dream and live there, she couldn't. Everything was wrong. Sam didn't understand her truth. He was blinded to the reality of who she was. She wasn't the kind of woman a man built a life with, and after all that Sam had been through with Lindsay, he deserved better. Something in him seemed to yearn for a white-picket-fence kind of life, and it was likely the mix of his failed marriage, his time in the military and the childhood he had never spoken to her about.

Amy's life was destined to be lived in secret, never secure, always looking over her shoulder. Sam couldn't stay in his calling with the marshals and settle down with her wherever she landed next. It would be impossible.

God, why? She pressed her forehead tighter against her knees until her head throbbed. Why would God bring her a man like Sam when she couldn't be with him? When she was no better than her mother, searching for a fairy tale?

And no matter what Sam said, she couldn't forgive herself for what she'd done. Maybe Jesus could, but she wasn't Jesus. She had no lens through which to see herself other than her own, and it was faulty. And what she saw was a guilty woman, one who was responsible for dozens of blackmail and trafficking victims. One who should have opened her eyes and realized what was happening sooner.

You did what was right as soon as you found out what was going on. How could you have known sooner what Meyer and Cutter were up to?

Amy lifted her head, replaying Sam's words, really inspecting the past for the first time since she'd left El Paso. How could she have known sooner? Grant had kept a set of coded books separate from the main accounts Amy worked with at the spa. She'd have never known they existed if Layla hadn't told her about them. Everything she'd learned had come from Layla, who'd trusted her enough to tell her the truth, who had trusted Amy with her life.

One tear ran down her cheek, followed by

another. It was as though Sam's words had unlocked something she didn't know she'd hidden away. She'd sought God's forgiveness over and over, and she knew He told the truth in the Bible. If she truly believed the way she claimed, then she trusted the sacrifice Jesus had made on her behalf. She was forgiven, and she'd do well to accept forgiveness from Him as well as from herself.

Could she truly forgive herself? Was there really freedom for her instead of condemnation?

"There is therefore now no condemnation to them which are in Christ Jesus."

The words were nearly as clear as if they'd been spoken aloud. Condemnation. She'd been punishing herself, insisting she deserved to be punished, which meant Christ's sacrifice equaled nothing in her life.

The bottom fell out of her pain and nearly stole her breath. She'd been living a lie in more ways than one. The worst kind of lie, refusing to believe that Jesus could forgive her.

Oh, God. I am so, so sorry. For the first time in her life, she understood grace. She didn't get what she deserved. She got to be free.

The front door of the cabin slammed shut,

drawing her into the present, into a lighter feeling and a clearer view of not only herself but of the world. Amy pressed her hands against the floor and shoved herself up along the door, then wiped her face with the hem of her sweatshirt.

The hem of *Sam's* sweatshirt. It even smelled like him, like that something she'd come to identify with him over the past few months, a scent that lingered in her apartment long after he and Edgecombe left after their meetings.

It nearly made her cry all over again, but she swallowed the tears and faced the door. She might not be able to tell him how she felt, that he'd taken another piece of her heart with him every time she'd seen him, but she could tell him she understood what he had been telling her earlier…that she wasn't to blame. That she was forgiven.

She turned the knob gently and pulled the door open a sliver, peering through the crack to make certain the mysterious Rich was gone.

Sam was alone in the room, sitting on the couch with his head in his hands. He stared at the floor and didn't seem to hear Amy as she pulled the door the rest of the way open and eased into the living area.

When she stepped forward, one of the floorboards creaked under her foot, alerting him to her presence.

Sam lifted his head, then stood, watching her warily as though he thought she might be about to unleash another arrow at him. He shoved his hands in his pockets, a gesture of uncertainty she wasn't used to seeing in him.

She'd done this to him, had made him feel off balance by aiming for his jugular with that comment earlier, before she'd stormed out and shut the door on him. The thought that she'd caused him pain stuck in her chest, a pain she wasn't sure how to dislodge. She only knew she had to make it right in the best way she could. Swallowing her pride, she shoved her hands into the pockets on the front of his sweatshirt and forced herself to look him in the eye. "I'm sorry. What I said earlier..." She raised her eyebrows and tried to give him a reassuring smile that likely looked more like a grimace. "You were right, and I was wrong. I was self-centered, only seeing things from my point of view, punishing myself and refusing to see that anyone else was involved or that anyone else was hurting."

Sam stared at her, seeming to read something in her posture or in her expression. Finally, he stepped around the coffee table and walked toward her, each step he took echoing in her heartbeat. Faster. "No, you were right. I wasn't doing a great job of forgiving myself either." The look in his eye matched the expression he'd worn before, both at his headquarters and only a few moments before.

It was a look that said he wasn't going to be content with being her protector or her friend. A look that said she could have everything she dreamed with him...if circumstances were different.

No matter either of their feelings, she was a witness and he was a marshal. She'd be someone new by next week and he'd still be Sam saving the world.

When he stopped in front of her, he looked down at her but didn't reach for her.

It didn't matter. His presence was enough. Amy forgot everything that mattered. There was only Sam. Only this moment and this cabin.

Maybe they could successfully hide out in this cabin from the world forever. After all, no one knew they were here.

She dipped her chin away from Sam, not

wanting to meet his eye. She could hide forever but he couldn't. He had a life, and it involved saving other people who weren't her. She squared her shoulders, bolstering herself to make the hardest speech of her life. "Sam, we should probably talk about—"

"Get down!" Sam grabbed her by the wrist and dragged her behind him, reaching for the gun at his hip in the same motion. "Someone's at the window."

Glass shattered behind Amy as Sam shoved her toward the living room. She whirled as she stumbled, catching herself on the arm of the horrible flowered sofa. The window near the kitchen was gone. A shadow moved outside, and a large gray object flew through the window, landing in the center of the room between her and Sam. It hummed and buzzed, throwing off bits of black shrapnel as it landed.

The buzz grew louder as the shrapnel grew thicker.

Not a bomb. Not shrapnel. Wasps. Amy cried out as the first sharp pain bit into her hand.

She stared at the welt as Sam called her name. Her ears rang. Dark spots danced before her eyes. Her throat itched and ached.

Amy dropped to the floor and curled into a ball, praying no more would sting her.

Her breath wheezed as the world darkened. She tried to cry out to Sam but nothing escaped her lips that were tingling and swelling. More stings didn't matter.

She was deathly allergic. One was enough to kill her.

Sam froze, staring at the huge wasp nest as Amy dropped to the floor. Self-preservation demanded he run.

Amy's presence demanded he stay. She cried out twice as he dove into the fray, reaching for the back of her sweatshirt to drag her out of the way. "Hang on. I've got you." He dragged her toward the open door to her bedroom, trying to outrace the stinging wasps. His wrist burned with a sting, and another quickly followed on his hand. While bees could kill him, he'd been stung by a wasp and never had a reaction to one. He prayed he wouldn't have one now.

But Amy…

I didn't even get to grab my go-bag or my EpiPen. She'd lamented the loss of her go-bag when he'd first picked her up and he'd teased her about keeping one. But she was without her epinephrine and his was on the couch in his own go-bag, a forest of wasps between them.

"Sam…" Amy's voice came to him, weak and slurred. "I got…" She tried to lift her hand and he saw it, the angry red welt on her palm. She'd been stung, and the way her words were slowing and her body weight growing heavier, she wasn't as blessed as he was.

She was allergic to wasps. He had to move fast.

As Sam reached her room and prepared to drag her inside and slam the door, Rich burst through the front door. "I heard the glass, but I was on the other side of the house and—" He muttered something and swatted the air. "What in the—"

Sam nearly collapsed in relief. Amy was fading fast. "Toss me my bag on the couch. Grab the two vests off of the chair and bring them." If they had to move out, he wanted Amy and him both in bulletproof vests as soon as they left the hospital. "Bring the truck around to the back to Amy's window. We're going to have to risk the hospital. We'll go through the window. She can't get stung again."

"I can try to catch who did this. They have

to be close." Rich slid the backpack across the floor.

"I need you behind the wheel." Sam slammed the bedroom door and smashed two more wasps crawling on his sweatshirt, the only thing protecting Amy from more stings.

She tried to ball up on the floor, her eyes never leaving Sam's face. Already, her lips were swelling. She tried to move her mouth, but nothing came out.

His first instinct was to pull her to him and comfort her, but that moment of comfort could cost her life.

Wrenching himself away from her, Sam tore open his backpack and dug through the main compartment, his fingers blessedly closing around the epinephrine injector. Popping the safety cap, he pulled back and drove the injector into Amy's thigh.

She flinched but didn't react otherwise. He held the injector in place for a few seconds, then pulled it out and tossed it aside. Sitting next to Amy, he drew her to his chest, praying frantically it would only take one injection to bring her around. He didn't have a second dose and he needed to be able to move her into Rich's truck. If she was dead weight, it would be harder.

And if the injection didn't work, she'd be dead before they ever reached a hospital. Her forty-two seconds were almost gone.

Gradually, her muscles took on her weight and Amy wasn't so heavy in his arms. The wheezing eased, but the shaking started. She shuddered against him as the epinephrine hit her system. At least she was breathing. But they had to move quickly. The injection could wear off. In spite of the risks involved in moving her while someone was clearly in the woods, he had to get her to an emergency room.

Outside the window, Rich parked the truck close to the house and jumped out. He opened the rear door, then turned and pounded on the window. Reluctantly, Sam laid Amy on the cot and shoved the window open. "Anyone out there?"

"Not that I can see. Either they're trying to flush you guys out or they figured the wasps would do the job. You holding up?" He scanned the area as he spoke, watching for movement.

Hefting Amy, Sam held her close. He rushed to the window. "You're going to be okay. We're getting you out of here."

"No. I'll be fine." She struggled slightly against him. "We can't leave here. It's not safe."

"And you're not in the clear." As Sam reached the window, Rich held out his arms to receive Amy. Sam drew her closer for a moment before he passed her to Rich. "I'm not losing you this way. We've got you." He held his breath as Rich took her, praying gunshots wouldn't fire from the woods. The angle Rich had parked the truck left little room for a shot, but still…

Still, he hadn't seen a wasp attack coming either. So clearly, he wasn't the best judge of the lengths Amy's would-be killer would take to destroy her.

Sam scrambled out the window and into the backseat of the truck, with Rich gunning the engine before Sam even had the door closed behind him. He buckled Amy and himself in as she sagged against him, praying they'd make it in time.

Praying his lack of vigilance hadn't killed her.

FIFTEEN

Amy blinked awake and tried to focus on something in the bright hospital room, but everything blurred together under the blinding lights. The beige walls, the gray tile floors, the white blanket… They swirled together into one big blob of nothing. She let her eyes slip shut again. It felt like hours since anything in her world had been clear. The last memory in focus was the sharp, burning sting as a wasp found her hand and delivered it's kill shot.

Everything since that moment—coming into consciousness in Sam's arms, the wild drive down the mountain to the hospital, her examination in the ER—it had all felt as though it had happened to someone else, someone who didn't live in her body. She'd have thought she was dreaming if not for the dull pain where the IV had been in her hand.

She'd drifted in and out, fighting to stay awake, preferring sleep, because it didn't hurt so bad or feel so disconnected. She groaned and tried to open her eyes again, praying it wouldn't hurt this time.

A shadow drifted over her, hovering. She eased one eye open and found Sam leaning over her. "Welcome back to the world, sleepy head."

"You're here." Her voice came out in a raspy whisper, her throat still aching from the swelling. Something in her mind had assumed that, now that she was out in the world, he would move on to the next assignment, would make the clean break that would hurt for a moment but would save them both a world of hurt in the long run. As her eyes adjusted to the light in the room, he came into focus, his brown eyes tired, dark circles beneath them. But he smiled at her and it erased his fatigue.

"I wouldn't dream of being anywhere else."

"You're okay?" He was allergic to bees too, and it had to have been his epinephrine that he'd injected her with at the cabin. It would be just like him to put her life ahead of his own. "You didn't react?"

"You don't have to talk. I know it hurts."

He brushed her hair from her forehead, following the motion of his hand with his eyes. "I'm only allergic to bees. Never reacted to a wasp. You, on the other hand, seem to have a sensitivity to both." He sat in a chair she hadn't noticed beside the bed and wouldn't meet her eye. "Seems our would-be killer is someone who knows you well and is using what they know to their advantage."

"I know them? Or Grant told them?" The information had been in her file at work, and she'd kept epinephrine with her at all times, even when she was working at the spa. "It could be anyone."

"Regardless, I missed this. I thought of guns, bombs, car chases… I never considered someone would toss a giant wasp's nest through a window to get to you. I knew you were allergic. It should have been on my list of—"

"Stop it." Amy lifted her hand, grimacing at the sharp ache in her joints, and held it out, inviting him to take it. When he gently laid his palm in hers, she wrapped her fingers loosely around his. "You couldn't have imagined this. You're human. You can't know everything. It's impossible."

"It's my job."

"To keep me alive. And you did." She squeezed his fingers. The room stopped its swirling and the shaking slowed to a dull hum deep in her insides. The medicine must be doing its job. The only other time she'd had to go to the ER, things had cleared up pretty quickly once the IV was in. But she wasn't important right now. Sam was. Her physical pain was no comparison to his emotional and spiritual wounds. She should know. Her freedom was so new, she could still feel the tenderness in her chest. "What was it you said to me at the cabin? That I had to forgive myself? Well, I have. It's time for you to follow your own advice."

Sam withdrew his hand from hers and sat back in the chair, crossing his arms. "I hear you. But as long as you're lying there as pale as the sheets, it's a little bit hard not to believe I bear the brunt of the responsibility."

"You can't—" A knock on the door stopped her argument and turned Sam's head.

A man she didn't recognize stuck his head in the door. His brown hair was slightly longer than military regulations would allow, and he sported a beard that was neatly trimmed yet covered the lower half of his face. This must be Rich.

Gray eyes flicked past her to Sam and he lifted a cell phone. "They're trying to call you. Signal's in and out."

Sam was on his feet and halfway to the door before she realized he was in motion. He wasn't leaving her here alone, was he? "Sam?" It would be a wonder if he could hear her feeble voice.

He stopped and pivoted toward her. "You're safe. Two Asher Creek police officers are outside the door. I'm coordinating for the Marshals Service to get here from Asheville. I'll be right outside. Since we're already in the open, I reached out to my team and they're getting back to me. I have to take this call." He stepped toward her, then stopped himself. "I'll be right back. I promise."

Before she could argue, he disappeared out the door with Rich close behind.

Amy turned her face to the wall. He was in contact with his team. She was out in the world again and he would turn her over to the regular team now, a team of marshals who would escort her to Washington, DC, and relocate her somewhere else in the country. If they couldn't figure out who was behind the resurgence of Grant Meyer's organization, then she was destined to spend the rest of her life as another person. Only this time it would be so much worse, because her new identity wouldn't include Sam. She'd already lost so much—including her twin sister—but losing Sam would cut so much deeper than anything else.

Voices outside the door turned her head, but none of the three belonged to Sam. Two deeper male voices and a female voice laughing with them. Probably the police officers and a nurse.

Sure enough, there was a light tap at the door and a cheery "Knock, knock!" A nurse in gray scrubs slipped in and carefully shut the door behind her. Her chestnut hair was knotted at the base of her neck and there was something familiar about the way she stood.

Amy pushed herself up slightly. The woman reminded her of...

The nurse turned and faced Amy, leaning back against the door with a slight smile on her face.

"Layla?" What? How had the other woman found her? Had she relocated here? Become a nurse? Was it a huge coincidence that Amy had landed in the same hospital as the woman she'd rescued from a life of trafficking and helped to hide from both the authorities and Grant Meyer?

It didn't matter. Relief robbed her muscles and made her feel weak all over again. Layla was safe after all. She may have disappeared when Amy had tried to locate her before, but she was safe. "You're okay." She rasped the words, wishing they were louder.

"I'm fine. Always have been." Her dark eyes scanned the room. "You're by yourself?"

"For now." Maybe forever, if Sam was immediately reassigned. The thought that she might never see him again, that he might move on without her getting the chance to tell him how she felt almost chocked her as much as the wasp venom had. But she had more pressing things to focus on. Layla was here. It should bring her joy. Instead, Layla's unexplained appearance set her stomach churning. Or maybe it was a side effect of her day.

She watched as Layla pushed away from the door and strode toward the bed, her eyes searching Amy's. She punched some buttons on the IV machine.

Amy watched. Did Layla work here? Wouldn't that be a huge coincidence? "How did you find me?"

"Easy." When she reached the bedside, Layla lifted Amy's wrist and tapped the face of the watch she'd put on only a couple of days earlier. "You led me right to you."

Amy's eyebrows drew together. The watch? Nothing made sense. The wasp venom and the epinephrine must be doing a number on her brain. "I don't understand. You were looking for me?"

"Ever since WITSEC offed you in El Paso. Nice ruse there, making everyone think you died in a car accident. It was a little bit too convenient, but I nearly believed it. I'm sure Grant did too, for a minute."

"I'm sorry." She'd never wanted to cause anyone pain, not Layla, not her sister, not any of her friends or coworkers in Texas. "I tried to find you, to warn you that Grant—"

"I knew what he was doing. I also knew he wound up in jail. He was stupid, getting caught going after your twin sister. I thought he was smarter than that."

The things Layla was saying… It was almost as though she knew everything, had been following the whole situation. It was almost as though she knew more than Amy did. Fear zipped through her, though she couldn't explain why. There was no reason to be afraid of Layla. She'd been the one to point Amy in the direction of Grant and Logan's crimes in the first place.

Her expression must have shown her doubt, because Layla's fingers tightened around her wrist, digging in. "If you'd put on the watch sooner, I'd have found you sooner."

"What?" Why did she keep talking about the watch? "You're hurting me."

"Not for long." Layla glanced at the door, then pulled a water bottle from her pocket. "If I remember correctly, you have a serious allergy not only to bees but to bee pollen." She kept one hand wrapped tightly around Amy's wrist while she unscrewed the cap on the water bottle with the index finger and thumb of the other hand. "Bad enough that given your already weakened state, it could kill you." She smiled down at Amy.

Amy's heart beat faster and a painful shot of adrenaline hit her bloodstream. She tried to fight but her body rebelled in its exhaustion. Fear and residual pain trapped her voice in her throat.

"You and Anthony are my last loose ends, Amy. Thank you for believing in my innocence and helping me disappear and avoid the authorities and their questions all those years ago. It made it so much easier to keep the organization running while Grant was hiding."

Faster than Amy could follow, Layla let go of her wrist and grabbed her jaw, squeezing her mouth open and pouring water in. Amy choked and gagged, trying to turn her head, but Layla was relentless. Water forced its way down her throat.

The reaction was immediate. Her lips tingled. Her throat ached and swelled. Bee pollen. In the water. *No.*

Layla stepped back, poured a cup of water from the pitcher beside the bed, took a sip, then laid the cup by Amy's hands. "They really should have kept you on that epinephrine drip a little longer."

As she headed for the door, Amy wheezed and choked, fighting for breath as the world faded to black.

Sam pressed Send on the phone then leaned against a window at the end of the hallway and glanced toward Amy's room. The two police officers still stood guard. The nurse they'd admitted when Sam left slipped out and walked in his direction. She stopped, smiled at him, then checked her watch and turned on one heel toward the nurse's station. Probably forgot to make notes.

Beside him, Rich also watched the hallway, although no one was in view except nurses and doctors. He pushed away from the wall. "I'm going to go sit with Amy while you make the call." He walked off in the direction of the nurse's station, pausing by Amy's door to speak to the police officers. He reached out to open the door, then stopped and stepped back to continue chatting with the officer on the right.

Sam glanced at his own watch. It had only been three or four minutes since he'd left Amy, but he was antsy to get back. He'd wandered farther from her door than he'd wanted, but he hadn't been able to get a good signal in the hall. Hopefully, here by the window, he'd be able to hear what Dana's broken message had been trying to tell him.

She answered on the first ring. "Sam!"

"I couldn't get a signal. I think we're good now. Listen, I need—"

"Sam, where are you?"

"At the hospital with Amy." Even though he was making contact, he was leery of giving an exact location over Rich's unsecured cell phone. "She was attacked by—"

"Get her secure. We know who's after her."
Dana was more no-nonsense than he'd ever
heard her be. "We've been trying to locate
you and, since I remembered to write the
debit card number down, tracked your usage
of the card to follow you as far as the hotel
fire outside of Franklin. We managed to get
security footage."

Sam straightened, already walking toward
Amy's room. He'd have to move her, but he
wasn't sure how and even if she was in any
condition to be moved. They'd pulled her epinephrine, so maybe he could get her somewhere secure. Now that he had his team back
online, his options were wide open. "What
did you find?"

"There were two people in the hotel on the
floor you guys were on after the alarm went
off. A man and a woman. Both armed. The
woman looked straight at the camera as they
breached the door of the room next to yours."

Amy's room. They'd known where she was
all along. "Do we know her?"

"Not yet. We picked up the male suspect
not too far from the hotel. He's a gun-for-hire
and claims he doesn't know who the woman
is, just that she offered him a nice chunk of
change to help her out. I've got a still of the

video running through facial rec and am waiting for a hit, but that takes time. On a hunch, I ran her face against surveillance photos from one of Grant Meyer's spas, the one where Amy worked. She's a match. I've sent the photo to the number you're calling from. Be on the lookout for her. She's one of your bad guys."

So it really was someone who knew Amy personally. Sam pulled the phone away and glanced at the screen, but the message hadn't come in yet. Rich's phone only had one bar, barely enough to hang onto this phone call. "I'm waiting. Anything else?"

"Not right now, but be careful and be on the lookout. Whoever this woman is, she doesn't seem to have a lot of muscle behind her or she wouldn't be hiring locals to do her dirty work, but she's definitely determined."

"Call me at this number the minute you get more. I'll be in touch." As he killed the call, the phone dinged with an incoming text.

Sam pulled it up to find a split screen image. One shot of a woman in the hallway of their hotel, one at the entrance to New Horizons Day Spa.

Both of them showed the same nurse who had exited Amy's room only a moment before.

He broke into a run, shouting for Rich as he pulled his weapon. "Go! Go get that nurse. Now!"

Without asking for a reason, Rich broke away from his conversation with the police officer outside of Amy's door and took off in the direction of the nurse's station. The other officer followed. Sam prayed the woman hadn't created herself a cushion that gave her enough of a head start to get away from them in the small hospital.

Brushing past the remaining police officer, Sam burst into Amy's room with the cop on his heels.

Amy's face was swollen and red. Water soaked her hospital gown and the sheets across her chest. Her lips were tinged blue.

No, no, no. Sam leaned over her, feeling for a pulse, listening for breath. She wheezed softly, her pulse rapid and thready. She was still with them.

He whirled to the officer who'd come in behind her. "Get a doctor. A crash cart. Something. She's relapsed." Not relapsed. She'd been attacked. Again. Under his nose.

Forty-two, forty-one...

SIXTEEN

Amy blinked her eyes open, a strong sense of déjà vu sweeping through her. She'd been here before. Had done this exact thing before. If she turned her head to the left, Sam would be beside her, watching over her.

She blinked against the dim light and shifted her head to find Sam sitting exactly where she'd known he'd be, relief slacking the muscles in his face as he took in a deep breath of what had to be relief. "Welcome back to the world, sleepy head."

He'd definitely said that before. How was she here again? There had been wasps stinging her, Sam dragging her across the floor, the hospital...

Layla.

Amy struggled, trying to sit up, fighting the IV in her hand. She had to run. To flee. It was Layla. Layla wanted her dead.

"Hey, hey, hey." Sam stood and rested his hands on her shoulders, gently easing Amy against the pillows. When she'd calmed, he pressed the button and raised the head of the bed slightly so she didn't feel so vulnerable and helpless. As her head lifted, her heart rate eased and the clinching in her chest eased, allowing her to breathe. "It's Layla, Sam." Her voice rasped against residual swelling. "Layla's trying to kill me."

"We know." He slipped his hand under hers. "Dana found security footage of her at the hotel and we saw her coming out of your room. Rich and one of the police officers who was guarding your door caught up to her as she tried to flee the hospital. She's in custody. She force-fed you water loaded with bee pollen." He grimaced, then gifted her a gentle smile. "You'll be fine. I doubt you remember, but the nurses got you cleaned up so there wouldn't be any residual issues. You're going to be fine."

As the fight for survival eased, the sense of betrayal swept in, a tidal wave that flooded her emotions. Tears pressed against the backs of her eyes, threatening to spill down her cheeks. Amy turned her head away from

Sam. The pain of her friend's treachery hurt worse than any ache in her body.

"You okay?" Sam's voice was heavy with compassion, maybe even pity.

She'd never been one who desired pity. It was the worst thing anyone could do to her. But she needed answers. "Why?"

Sam's fingers tightened around hers. "She fooled everyone, not just you. Dana shot me some info while you were sleeping. Turns out Layla isn't even her real name. It's Sienna Burgaw and she has a record longer than your arm. And despite what she told you, she wasn't in the country illegally."

"Then why did she want to hide from the investigators? Why did she lead me to all of the information on Grant and Logan?"

His thumb ran a lazy circle on the soft skin of her wrist, the feeling the touch brought completely incongruous to her emotions. "Sienna Burgaw was an underling working for Meyer and Cutter, keeping an eye on things from the inside, making sure no one got too close, but she got greedy. She saw a way to shut them down while keeping their operation running and the money going into her pocket, so she tipped you off, had them both outed to the authorities, and there was no indication to either of them that she was behind it. She fed you the story about being an illegal and afraid of the authorities, so you hid her pretty well. No one suspected. Meyer and Cutter assumed you stumbled on the information and went after you, which would have eliminated you as her source. She had Cutter murdered several months ago before he could put things together, and she started tying up loose ends immediately after, letting Meyer come after you. When he was arrested, he was a liability who could rat her out if he thought it would get him a reduced sentence, so she had him murdered. She was smarter than all of them. Her last two loose ends were you and Anthony."

"Anthony." She tried to sit up but Sam eased her back down. "Is he okay?"

"He's fine. Dana's been in contact with him and our people in El Paso have moved him into hiding until we're certain we've tied up all of the loose ends with Burgaw and her new organization."

Amy sank against the pillows, her energy flagging. It sounded as though everyone was safe and she could move on to her new life without leaving anyone behind her in danger. But the thought of leaving Sam was growing harder by the second. It couldn't be stopped, but she needed to know he wouldn't beat himself up forever over letting Layla get to her. "Don't blame yourself."

"About that…" Sam smiled, squeezed her hand, then let go to relax in the chair. "I had a lot of time to think while you were playing Sleeping Beauty just now. And you're right. Well, what I said to you was right, so I guess that means I'm right. Right?" He shot her a wink that nearly weakened her muscles more than the ordeal of the past few hours. "No one saw this Layla/Sienna person coming. Nobody. Same with the wasps. Same with…" His voice faded, and he stared at the wall behind her for a moment before he cleared his throat. "Someone was killed on my watch, but I couldn't have seen it coming either. I tried my best, just like I've tried my best with you. And beating myself up repeatedly for things outside of my control when I know I've done my best is wrong. It's a sin. It negates what Jesus did on the cross. So you're right. I'm right. It's time to let go and accept some grace as well as giving some to myself." This time when he smiled, it seemed freer, easier than she'd ever seen it before. "It's time to learn from my mistakes instead of living in them."

Amy smiled. He'd learned the same thing she had. And while she might never be free to be Amy Brady again, never free to be with the man she now realized she loved, she was free in every way that mattered even more than that.

Sam's smile shifted from joy into one that looked to be slightly mysterious. "There's something else we need to talk about."

Amy raised an eyebrow. "Okay…"

"Grant Meyer and Logan Cutter are dead. Sienna Burgaw is in custody and is talking already, probably hoping for a reduced sentence. She's not the strong crime boss she wants to pretend she is. Once we know the whole of her organization is shut down…"

As he trailed the thought off, the implications of his words were slow to sink in, but as they registered, they brought an entirely different kind of muscle weakness. "I might be free?" This time, the scratch in her voice was more the product of unshed tears than the beating her body had taken through the day.

"I can't make you any promises, but it's looking like a greater possibility every moment." This time, when he took her hand, he gripped it as though he never wanted to let go. "It would be your choice, of course. No one knows what Sienna Burgaw will try or if she will be as vengeful as Grant Meyer was and that's a chance you'd be taking, but with the way she's behaving now… She might have been one seeking a ruthless climb to the top, but she certainly doesn't want to pay the piper in full. I'd imagine her criminal days are done once she's behind bars."

Amy nodded and gripped his hand. "I could see my sister?" Her twin might not forgive her, but at least Amy had to try. She prayed that blood and their history together as close sisters would cover the multitude of her sins.

"You sure?"

"Grace. I'm going to rely on grace. Same way you should."

"I'm working on it, and on that note, maybe there's something else we should talk about." This time, when his expression shifted, it held something like a veiled fire. "When you're a free woman, I think we should—"

A knock on the door stopped whatever he'd planned to say, and Isaiah peered inside. His gaze landed on Amy first, and he gave her a slight smile as he stepped into the room. "Nice to see you looking healthy."

"Nice to be healthy." She glanced at Sam, silently begging him to look at her again the way he had been before they were interrupted. "Your team's here?"

Sam nodded, but he was watching Isaiah. "Is it time?"

"A couple of minutes. Everything is in place." He gave a quick nod, then disappeared again as the door slipped closed behind him.

"Wait." Amy's eyebrows furrowed, bringing the dull ache in her head into clearer focus. "What's happening?"

"We still have to get you to a safe place until we know for certain the threat to your life is over. We're moving you to a secure ward in the hospital where we can control who comes and goes until you're well enough to travel, and then you'll be moved to DC." Sam turned toward her again, his gaze full force on hers, holding her into place and sending her mind and heart whirling to places she wasn't certain she was ready to handle. "Before we move you and there are people watching you around the clock, I want to—"

Another knock, and a nurse stepped in pushing a wheelchair.

Everything was happening so fast. Amy was free but she wasn't. She had Sam but she didn't. She was safe but she was in danger. Her head throbbed too much to make sense

of anything happening other than one thing…
Sam had something to say and no one was
letting him say it. She needed to know what
it was, craved the knowledge that his feelings
for her mirrored hers for him.

But he slipped away from her with a look of
defeat, not meeting her eye again as he helped
the nurse ease her into the wheelchair. When
she was settled, he led the way to the door
with the nurse pushing the chair.

Every inch closer to the door crushed the
air from her chest even harder. If they made
it to the hallway, Sam might morph back into
a government agent and never again take the
risk of saying the words she'd seen behind his
eyes. "Wait. Stop."

The nurse hesitated, but Sam was all motion, stopping in front of the chair and pre-
venting any further motion toward the door.

He knelt in front of Amy and searched her
eyes before he glanced at the nurse. "Can you
give us a second?" The other woman hesitated, but when Sam shot her a look that said
he meant business, she hurried from the room
and shut the door behind her.

The nurse's exit hardly registered with Sam
as Amy lifted her free hand and ran her fin-

gers down his cheek. The gesture was the only confirmation he needed. Letting his cheek rest against her palm, he reached up, slid her palm to his mouth and planted a kiss in the center. "If I don't get you upstairs in about two minutes, a bunch of deputy marshals are going to show up to escort you to a safe place. While I'm almost certain that's going to be temporary, I can't let it happen before I say what needs to be said. And if I don't say it quick, we're probably going to be interrupted again so…" Sam slid his hand up her arm and across her shoulder to tangle his fingers in the hair at the base of her neck. He drew her closer until their foreheads nearly touched and whispered, "I will come for you no matter where WITSEC sends you next. And I will never leave."

Amy leaned into him, her expression seeming to melt at his touch.

"I might have yelled at you the first time I found you, when you were brash enough to duck out of WITSEC, but I think I also started falling in love with you in that moment. It's why I stayed close to you and partnered with Edgecombe."

"I thought they ordered you."

"I asked."

"I'm glad." She tipped her head and brushed her lips against his, then backed away slightly. "I love you."

"I was supposed to say that first." He was dying to kiss her, to seal this moment with a kiss neither of them would ever forget, but he had one more thing to say, one more thing he had to know before he could let go and fully give his heart to her forever in a way he'd never imagined he'd be free to do. "I have an idea for your new name."

Confusion flitted across her features and she stiffened. "I thought you said I was about to be free of all of this."

"I'm thinking Amy Maldonado has a nice ring to it."

As the realization of what he was asking dawned, a smile tipped the corners of her mouth. "It's perfect." Without waiting for him to make the move, she closed the small space between them, kissing him in a way that no one else ever had, pouring herself into him and healing the last of his broken places.

She started a new clock in his heart, one that counted up to a lifetime with her.

EPILOGUE

She could do this. She could do this. She could do this.

Amy pressed her back against the sun-warmed brick beside the window of The Color Café in the tiny downtown of Mountain Springs, North Carolina. Her heart threatened to beat a path up her throat, choking off her oxygen. *Could* she do this? Could she walk the five feet to the door, pull it open and face her twin sister for the first time in too many years?

Leaning against the wall beside her, Sam laced his fingers through hers and squeezed, the pressure of the ring he'd presented to her when she left the hospital the day before still new—and glorious—on her finger. "Jenna's about to come out of her skin waiting for you to show up. You have nothing to be afraid of. It was all we could do to keep her from coming to the hospital, even though we told her over and over that you didn't want a reunion in a sterile room." He slipped his fingers from hers, then placed his hands on her shoulders and turned her gently toward the door. "Rich is probably having to call up all of his high school football moves to keep her from barreling out the door and searching for you."

Amy stiffened her neck and lifted her chin. Sam was probably right, and her sister was probably as excited for this reunion as Amy was herself. But still, that nagging fear that Eve—now Jenna—would turn her away was almost too much to overcome. Sam's fingers tightened on her shoulders and he leaned closer, his chest brushing her back and his whisper tickling her ear. "You can do this. I'm praying for you."

There it was. Truth. The tension eased and Amy pulled in her first deep breath since... since ever. This wasn't in her hands; it was in God's. He'd already seen how this would turn out. He already knew how her sister would greet her. Sam was right. There really was nothing to fear...

Even if everything inside of her was jumping and humming.

With a final quick prayer of her own, she

made the last steps to the door and pulled it open, stepping into the warmth of a bright, cheerful room filled with blank canvases and a range of artwork. The scent of paint and coffee mingled into a blend that was oddly comforting and somehow familiar.

She'd barely taken it in when a motion to the left caught her attention. She was half turned when her sister nearly tackled her, pulling her into a tight hug that Amy immediately and instinctively reciprocated. The tears came for them both, shaking their shoulders.

Relief and that final sense of *home* washed over Amy as she clung to the sister she'd been certain she'd never see again, embracing a life God had restored to her in ways she'd never imagined. A new town, a new love, a new beginning…but her family restored and her heart made whole.

Amy Brady was alive once again.

* * * * *

If you enjoyed this story,
look for Jenna's story,
Mistaken Twin.

Dear Reader,

Thank you so much for being a part of this three-book journey in the town of Mountain Springs…and in Jenna and Amy's reunion. I've had the best time weaving together Erin and Jenna and Amy's stories.

The common thread for them is fear. Isn't it amazing how often God has told us in the Bible not to fear? He knew from Creation that we would be afraid. There is so much to fear in this world. But here's the thing… Fear comes when we forget the One Who created us is the One Who is in control. That's true for me. When I begin to doubt, I pull a Peter, put my eyes on the waves and sink. The beauty happens when I, like Peter, cry out, "Lord, save me!" He always stretches out His hand and lifts me up.

I pray you know Jesus in that way. That those things you fear are things you can lay at His feet. As one who battled debilitating fear for a decade, I know it is not easy, but when I look back on those years, I see Jesus more than I see fear. Lift your head and seek Him. I promise He is there.

I'd love to hear from you!

Pop over to www.jodiebailey.com or send an email to jodie@jodiebailey.com. Hearing from you all always makes the day a bit brighter!

Jodie Bailey